Praise for *The SideRoad Kids*

"Sharon Kennedy gives us a peek into life in Michigan's Upper Peninsula in the 1950s. It was a simpler, less hectic time when kids like Katie, Blew, Squeaky, and Daisy grew up on farms instead of high rises and used their imagination instead of fancy gadgets to make their own fun. An entertaining read for youngsters. And parents, you might enjoy a nostalgic flashback as well. I know I did."

—Allia Zobel-Nolan, Author of *Cat Confessions*

"The stories in *The SideRoad Kids* are often humorous. However, underlying them is a sensitive awareness that being a kid, rural or urban, then or now, is not easy. This is an enjoyable read that will enlighten today's kids about the past and rekindle memories for readers who grew up in the late 1950s."

—Jon Stott, author of *Paul Bunyan in Michigan*

"Over the years, I've read many of Sharon Kennedy's stories. She's an amazing writer who draws you into the lives of her characters and keeps everything relatable. Readers can easily recall similar experiences. She makes you laugh, makes you think, and makes you want to keep reading. *The SideRoad Kids* is an entertaining book about a group of children growing up in Northern Michigan."

—Kortny Hahn, Senior Staff Writer, *Cheboygan Daily Tribune*

"Sharon's stories capture the essence of childhood and growing up in a small community. The antics of *The SideRoad Kids* will keep you entertained and take you back to a simpler time. Some of the stories were published in our magazine and were well received by adult readers."

—Renee Glass, Senior Production Artist, *Mackinac Journal*

The SideRoad Kids:

Tales from Chippewa County

Sharon M. Kennedy

Illustrations by Joanna Walitalo

Modern History Press

Ann Arbor, MI

The SideRoad Kids: Tales from Chippewa County
Copyright © 2021 by Sharon M. Kennedy. All Rights Reserved.
Illustrations by Joanna Walitalo

ISBN 978-1-61599-603-2 paperback
ISBN 978-1-61599-604-9 hardcover
ISBN 978-1-61599-605-6 eBook

Published by
Modern History Press   www.ModernHistoryPress.com
Ann Arbor, MI 48105   info@ModernHistoryPress.com

Distributed by Ingram (USA/Canada), Bertram's Books (UK/EU)

Library of Congress Cataloging-in-Publication Data

Names: Kennedy, Sharon M., 1947- author.
Title: The sideroad kids : tales from Chippewa County / Sharon M. Kennedy.
Description: Ann Arbor, MI : Modern History Press, [2021] | Audience: Ages
   10-12. | Audience: Grades 4-6. | Summary: Katie, Daisy, Blew, Shirley,
   and the other young kids who live in the farms along a sideroad in
   Chippewa County of Michigan's Upper Peninsula in the mid 1950s deal
   with the problems of growing up in their poor, isolated community in this
   collection of short stories.
Identifiers: LCCN 2021037309 (print) | LCCN 2021037310 (ebook) | ISBN
   9781615996032 (paperback) | ISBN 9781615996049 (hardcover) | ISBN
   9781615996056 (adobe pdf) | ISBN 9781615996056 (kindle edition)
Subjects: LCSH: Nineteen fifties--Juvenile fiction. | Farm
   life--Michigan--Chippewa County--Juvenile fiction. | Chippewa County
   (Mich.)--History--20th century--Juvenile fiction. | CYAC: Farm
   life--Michigan--Fiction. | Chippewa County (Mich.)--History--20th
   century--Fiction. | LCGFT: Historical fiction.
Classification: LCC PZ7.1.K5055 Si 2021   (print) | LCC PZ7.1.K5055
   (ebook)
   | DDC 813.6 [Fic]--dc23
LC record available at https://lccn.loc.gov/2021037309
LC ebook record available at https://lccn.loc.gov/2021037310

With love to Stephanie

Acknowledgements

I must first acknowledge my parents, Al and Ann Kennedy, who never complained when I asked for money to buy more books. To my paternal grandmother, the late Julia Kennedy, who always tucked a dollar in my hand to buy another *Nancy Drew* book. To my 10th grade English teacher, Eugene Buckley, who introduced me to Charles Dickens. To my English college professor, the late Mike Flynn, who said my work was "a golden vein of talent waiting to be mined." To my Detroit friend, the late George Mallus, who called my writing "beautiful." To Richard Crofton, the first editor to publish my newspaper column in the Sault News and some of my stories in the *Mackinac Journal*. To Victor Volkman who published this book. And to readers who hold my work in their hands. I acknowledge and thank all of you. Without your faith in me, these stories would never have been written.

Contents

Chapter 1 – Riding with Fenders

"Katie, telephone. Daisy wants to talk to you," Mama calls from the bottom of the stairs. I'm lying in bed, on top of the covers, reading *Little Women*. I'm at the good part where Laurie tells Jo he loves her.

"What's she want?" I yell. "Tell her I'm busy."

"Katie, come to the phone. Make up with Daisy. You're not doing anything that can't wait, and I won't lie for you. Daisy? Katie will be here in a minute."

I save my place by putting a bookmark between the pages. The last thing I want to do today is talk to Daisy. I'm mad at her. She stole my Annie Oakley canteen and won't give it back.

"What do you want?" I ask in the meanest voice I have. "What's up? I'm reading a good book."

"Fiddlesticks on your old book. Fenders wants to take us for a ride. He's waiting in the car. Call Blew and be here in ten minutes or we'll leave without you." Slam. She hangs up in my ear. I crank my cousin's number—three shorts and one long. The operator answers.

"This is the operator," she says.

"I don't want you. I cranked three shorts and one long." The line goes dead, and I try again. We were the second family on our road to get phone service this summer. Now everybody has it, but the Brimley phone company hasn't worked out all the bugs. Grandpa says it's faster to stand on the front porch and yell than it is to call. He says when the wind's from the right direction, our voices carry quicker on it than they do through the wires. I think he's right, but then I hear Blew's voice.

"Want to go for a ride? Fenders will take us wherever we want to go because Mr. Powell is selling the car tomorrow and this will be our last trip."

"Where we goin'?" Blew asks. "I'm playin' cowboys and Indians. I got all my men lined up for battle. I'll have to put 'em away if I go so the drive better be worth the trouble it's gonna cause me."

"I don't know. Maybe Cedarville. That's where we were headed last time, remember, but then we got the flat tire."

"We never even left the field. We didn't go nowhere."

"Well, I'm going today whether or not you are. Mama says I have to make up with Daisy. I'd rather eat a dead mouse." I slam the receiver in his ear just like Daisy did in mine. I know Blew won't miss a free ride. I run back upstairs and grab a sweater.

"Bye, Mama," I say as I dash through the kitchen and out the front door. I take my bike out of the red shed and start down the lane, Lard yapping at my heels. "You can't come," I scold him. "Stay home." Obediently, he trots back to the shade of the poplar tree where he was sleeping before he heard me. By the time I reach the end of my lane, I see Blew racing down the road ahead of me. I bet he wasn't playing cowboys and Indians at all. I bet he lied like he always does.

Fenders has driven at least a thousand miles. He drives everywhere. He's 18 and doesn't have many friends his own age so he often plays with us. He's already sitting behind the wheel when I pedal up the driveway. He waves and yells, "You're just in time."

We know the rules. Daisy sits in the front seat when we start our journey, and I sit there on the way back. Blew always sits behind Fenders and pretends he's driving. A map of Michigan is spread on Daisy's legs. It's an old map, torn and stained. Most of the new roads aren't on it, but it's good enough for us.

"Where we going?" I ask.

"Where do you want to go?" Fenders responds.

"I want to go to St. Ignace and see Castle Rock," Daisy says.

"I want to go to Point Iroquois Lighthouse and see where the Indians killed each other," Blew yells.

"I want to go to the fair and see the two-headed calf," I answer.

"And I want to go to the Soo and buy hamburgers at Dorothy's and eat them while we watch the freighters crawl through the locks," Fenders announces. "I know one of the guys

who works in the engine room of the *Leon Fraser*. It might be locking through today."

We sit in the car and stare at each other. We know we have to go where Fenders wants to go because he's the driver. Daisy folds the map, making sure she gets it just right and sticks it back in the glove box. We sure don't need a map to show us the way to Sault Ste. Marie. Our parents go there every Friday night. Our mamas go to the grocery stores, and our papas go to the beer gardens. I wish I'd stayed home.

"Who's gonna pay for burgers?" Blew asks. "You got any money, Fenders?"

"I got some."

"Enough for the four of us and gas?"

"Maybe yes. Maybe no. Don't worry about money."

"Why can't we go to the fair?" I ask. "It'll be over in three days."

"All summer you been promising to take me to Castle Rock," Daisy whines.

"C'mon, Fenders. Take us to the lighthouse," Blew demands. "Maybe we can find an old bloody tomahawk or some bones buried in the sand."

Fenders drums his fingers on the steering wheel like he's thinking. "I wonder how much gas we have. Blew, get a stick and shove it down the tank." Blew jumps out of the car and tears a twig from a maple tree. He strips the leaves from it, and sticks it in the gas hole. It's dripping when he pulls it out.

"Look here, we got lots of gas. Enough to get us to town and the lighthouse. We can watch the freighters from there. We've seen the locks a million times."

"Well," Fenders says. "You could be right but then again, you could be wrong. I don't have enough money for gas and food, and I don't like the idea of walking home if the tank runs dry. Blew says the tank's full, but we all know Blew's a liar. And he's broke. Either of you gals got any money?"

"No," Daisy and I say at the same time.

"Now, this does present a problem." Fenders scratches his head. "I want to take you kids for an end-of-the-summer ride, but we can't agree on where to go, and we don't have enough money to drive all over Chippewa County and grab some burgers, too. I don't want to disappoint anybody so we're going to have to compromise. Any of you know what that word means?"

"It means you're a liar," Blew grunts. "And we ain't goin' nowhere."

"Drive us to town, buy yourself a burger, then drive us to the lighthouse. I'll give up Castle Rock, if Katie'll give up the fair. I don't want to see no two-headed calf." Daisy barks out orders like my Grandpa.

"Give me time to think about that," Fenders says. He stretches his arms in front of him until they almost hit the windshield. It has a crack in it where a gravel truck hit it with sharp stones. Daisy turns and looks at me.

"I don't know why you're mad at me. I didn't steal your canteen," she says. "I found it. It was filthy so I washed it and brought it home. I'm not giving it back. You should take better care of your things." She turns around and looks out the window.

"I don't believe you, but Mama says I have to forgive you so I do." I don't really forgive her. What I really want to do is punch her in the nose. "You know I take excellent care of my things. I want my canteen back. You're a thief."

"Shut up, Katie," Blew says. "Ain't nobody listenin' to you. We ain't goin' nowhere today are we, Fenders? You're just teasin' us."

Fenders doesn't answer. He takes his wallet from his pocket and counts some bills. He gets paid for helping with farm chores, but I don't think he likes farm work. I think he wants to be a sailor like his friend. He always reads books about ships that sank in Lake Superior, the big lake a few miles from here. And every chance he gets, he goes to town with his dad and watches the freighters as they lock through on their way to Duluth or the St. Lawrence Seaway.

We sit in the car for what seems like an hour. Everybody's mad at everybody. Finally, Mrs. Powell comes out of the house carrying four lunch pails. She walks through the grass. "I thought you kids might like a sandwich and something to drink," she says. She walks around the car and hands each of us a pail. "I baked oatmeal cookies, but eat your peanut butter sandwiches first. There's cold milk in the thermoses. Enjoy." We thank her and dig in.

"Now that the food problem is solved, we'll decide where to go when we finish lunch," Fenders says. "Daisy, get out the map again. We'll go somewhere we've never been before. We'll have an adventure." Daisy hands him the map. He studies it for a long time.

"How about Soldier Lake out Raco way?" he suggests. "We haven't been there."

"I don't have a bathing suit," I say. "And everybody knows I can't swim."

"Good idea," Blew yells. "I'll swim in my underwear. Let's go."

"I'll run back to the house and wear my suit underneath my clothes. I'll grab some towels. Wait for me." Daisy limps away.

"Run fast," Fenders tells his sister, but she can't run fast because she has a club foot.

"You can walk in the woods and search for wildflowers," Fenders says to me. "When we're done swimming, we'll join you and look for different kinds of leaves. There's lots of trees out that way. C'mon, Katie. That calf will still be there next year."

"We both know that calf will be dead before Labor Day," I complain, but it's useless to argue. I finish eating my lunch. The cookie's good, but I don't like raisins so I pick them out and give them to Blew.

Now that we've settled on where we're going, a happy feeling fills the car. The thing is old. I can't imagine why anyone wants to buy it. It's mostly junk. The seats are ripped, the radio doesn't work, the locks won't lock properly, and the door on the driver's side won't open at all. Fenders has to slide across the seat to get in and out. The muffler drags on the ground. When the car was new it was dark green, but now there's almost more rust on it than paint.

When it quit running, the man at the Chevrolet store in Sault Ste. Marie wouldn't give Mr. Powell the price he wanted for it so he put one end of a chain on his tractor and the other end on the rear bumper of the car and dragged it into the field. It sat there until Fenders was old enough to tinker with it. Then he practiced driving. The first time we went on the road was thrilling. He made us close our eyes and pretend we were driving down US-2, heading for the ferry that would carry us across the Straits of

Mackinac. He said we were going to Detroit. We planned that trip for days, but we never left the field just like we won't today. The car has no roof and no engine. We go along with Fenders because it's fun to pretend. Daisy returns with the towels. "All set," she says. "Let's go."

"Close your eyes, kids, and hang on," Fenders tells us. "Next stop—Soldier Lake."

Chapter 2 – Statue Maker

"Freeze!" I shriek as I fling Daisy through the air. She lands on her right foot. "Freeze or the game's over."

"How can I freeze on my club foot?" she yells. She tumbles to the ground.

"Game's over then. I win."

"You always win, Katie, because you cheat. I'm going to tell Mommy."

"Big baby. Go and whine for all I care."

"Well, maybe I'll stay outside just a little longer."

"Good. If we're not going to play Statue Maker, let's watch Grandpa. I think he's been into Granny's dandelion wine so you'll probably have to cover your ears."

"I thought you said your papa made him promise to stay out of the wine and not say bad words." Daisy's eyes are wide with curiosity. "Do you lie as well as cheat?"

"I don't lie and I don't cheat. Be quiet and listen." We run towards the swings and start pumping. Grandpa rocked himself into a corner of the porch and can't reach his cane. It fell from his knees and rolled next to Lard.

"Katie, you lazy child. Help me out of this chair!" Grandpa yells. "And pick up my blasted cane!" He flings his drink at Lard. "Move, you blasted, mutt, move!"

Daisy is horrified. Her eyes bulge. "I've never heard anybody talk like that in all my life," she says.

I laugh. "If you came over more often, you'd know how he talks. All old people talk that way when they're mad."

"My people don't."

"You don't live with your grandpa." Before she has time to answer, her mother comes out of the house. I guess her visit is over. It's not really a visit because her mother sells Avon stuff, and

Mama always buys something. Mrs. Powell tells Daisy it's time to go.

"Maybe I'll see you tomorrow," she says, but she probably won't. She only comes over when her mother brings Mama whatever she bought. It's too hard for her to walk on the road or ride a bicycle. I jump from the swing.

"Bye, Daisy. See you tomorrow." She ignores me.

"Are you going to help me or not?" Grandpa hollers. I don't answer right away.

"I said are you going to help me?"

"Maybe I will. Maybe I won't. What'll you give me if I do?" I twist the end of my hair around my finger.

Grandpa narrows his eyes to cat-like slits. He lowers his head, sticks out his neck, and says very slowly, "If you don't give me that cane right this minute, I'll strangle you at midnight."

I laugh and perch on the top step of the porch. "If you strangle me, you'll go to jail. What'll people say then?"

"They'll say a poor old man was driven to madness by a demon-possessed child. They'll feel sorry for me and give me a prize."

I think about this for a minute. "Maybe yes. Maybe no. You'll still go to jail. You can't kill children and get away with it."

"You're not a child. You're a monster. A monster that came out of Lake Superior or Lake Michigan one stormy night."

"Oh, Grandpa. You say the funniest things. You don't even know what a monster looks like. And monsters don't live in the Great Lakes. Only the skeletons of sailors who sunk to the bottom with their ships live there. Besides, why do you want to go in the house? It's nice out here on the porch. Look at all the pretty red leaves on the maple tree." I twirl my hair with both hands.

"I'll strangle you with your own hair, that's what I'll do. I want to go inside because I'm tired. Tired and worn out," he says. "I'm ready for the bone pile. I'll probably never live to see another year." He drops his head low on his chin. "I'll never see another ripe garden or smell another red rose. I'll never taste another sweet blackberry or see the beautiful fall colors. Soon I'll be joining my dear old ma and pa."

"We don't have any roses or blackberries, and your ma and pa will be happy to see you. Besides, it's best to die when there's no snow. They bury you without waiting so it would be thoughtful of you to die now."

"Katie, give me that blasted cane."

"Why do you swear?"

"Give me the cane."

"Not until you answer me."

"My cane."

"When you die, can I have your cane? You won't need it anymore." Grandpa reaches for me but misses. I tell him I'll be right back. I want to get something from the kitchen. I stick my hand in the cookie jar and take out three chocolate chip cookies. Two for me and one for him. I push open the screen door.

"Grandpa, I'm sorry. I'll help you now. Here's a cookie and here's your cane. You won't really strangle me at midnight, will you?" He doesn't answer.

"You have to talk to me. Don't you want to talk to me? Don't you like me anymore?" I sit next to him. "Mama and Granny will get mad when I tell them you won't talk to me. Do you want them mad at you?" Grandpa still doesn't say a word. "I've tried to be your friend, but I guess you don't like me. I'm going to my playhouse." I set the cookie on the bench next to him. Then I kiss his cheek and run down the steps.

"Well, Lard," I hear him say. "It's time for us to go in."

"....he was just sitting there, not talking to me or anything. I didn't do anything to him. Honest, I didn't. I guess he was in one of his moods. You know how old people are." I chatter to myself in front of the mirror in my playhouse. I'm practicing what to say in case Grandpa tells on me. "I didn't do one little thing to make him mad. Honest I didn't. Not one little thing." The mirror doesn't answer me like the one in Snow White answered the queen, but I know what it's thinking. "Sometimes old people are nothing but trouble."

Chapter 3 – A Strange First Encounter

I met Shirley Quails when I was 11 years old. My name is Elizabeth. My family and had I had just moved into a pretty house in the country near a little town called Brimley in Michigan's Upper Peninsula. The salesman told Captain that a girl my age lived down the road. I waited for her to visit me, but she never did so a few days before school started, I rode my bike to her place. I pedaled against the wind and by the time I got to her house, I was angry.

Her mother was taking clothes off the line. She waved when she saw me and called a greeting. I got off my bicycle and walked over to the clothesline. Instead of shaking my hand or kissing my cheeks like some people do when they meet someone for the first time, she just said "hello" and continued filling the basket. When it was overflowing, she invited me in to meet her daughter. She said she had just baked a cake and when it cooled we could frost it and have cake and cold milk. I was afraid the milk had come from her cows. We don't get milk from the barn. We get it from the grocery store like you're supposed to. I followed her inside. What I saw scared me.

Her house wasn't like ours. There was no kitchen sink and no faucets. There was a little wooden stand with a white metal dish on it and a bar of soap next to it. Two pails filled with water were on a table by the back door. Something they called a "dipper" hung from a nail pounded into the wall. A towel hung from another nail. I was used to living in nice houses. I guess we were rich, although that thought never occurred to me until I stepped inside the Quails' house.

Shirley was sitting next to her grandmother on a cot in the kitchen. The cot looked like the grandmother's bed because a pillow and blankets were on it. A little stand was next to it with a

lamp, some books, and a ball of yarn with knitting needles stuck
in it. I later learned the grandmother always slept in the kitchen
not just during the day so she could be part of the activity but all
the time. I couldn't imagine a bed in the kitchen, but my
grandmothers were in heaven so I didn't know if all old ladies
preferred the kitchen to a room of their own.

"My name is Elizabeth," I said. "I'm your new neighbor. I've
come to make your acquaintance." I gave a little curtsey like
Momma taught me. I guess I was waiting for someone to applaud
or something but they didn't. The grandmother didn't say
anything, and Shirley stared at me like she was conducting an
inspection of someone from outer space. Then she asked if I had
any dolls.

"No, I don't like dolls," I said. "I like horses. Do you have any
horses?"

"No," she replied. "I don't like horses." I had never known
anyone in my life who didn't like horses. Our last home was on
Mackinac Island where everyone loves horses. I stared at Shirley
and she stared at me. I should have left immediately, but Momma
never allows me to eat sweets and that cake looked good so I
stayed.

Mrs. Quails finished making the frosting and handed a spoon
to Shirley and me. She told us to slather on as much chocolate as
we wanted and we did. Then we sat at the table and Mrs. Quails
cut a big slice for each of us. She opened the refrigerator and took
out a jar of milk. I knew perfectly well that milk had come from
the barn cows so I politely said I didn't want any when, of course,
I did. My throat was as dry as November leaves.

Shirley wasn't saying anything so I asked how many dolls she
had. She didn't answer right away. I sat on my chair and stared at
her. She wasn't like me. Her brown hair was braided like an old
lady's. She wore a plaid shirt and shorts. Her blue tenner shoes
were like mine, but hers were covered with grass stains. Her front
tooth was chipped. Her arms were long and her fingers were long
and her legs were long and her feet were long and from what I
could see everything was covered in long, brown hair except her
feet which were hidden by anklets and the tenners. I didn't want
to be her friend.

Finally she spoke. "I have seven dolls," she said. "They all have names. Do you want to know their names?"

"No," I said. "I have to go home." I had eaten my cake and was so thirsty I was almost tempted to drink the cows' milk.

"Do you want to go upstairs and meet my dolls?" she asked.

"No, I have to go home."

"Do you have to go home right now?" Shirley asked.

"Well, no, I guess not." I didn't really want to go home because Momma said I could stay for an hour and although I didn't have a watch, I knew the hour wasn't up yet. I didn't want to go upstairs in the creepy old house with the creepy girl, but I did.

Shirley walked in front of me. "I keep my dolls in the spare room above this room," she said. "It's our storage room." I followed her up the stairs. A rickety railing ran around them to the spare room. Shirley opened the door as if she were opening a door to a palace. Then she pulled a string dangling from the ceiling and a light came on.

"Here are my dolls," she said as if they were precious jewels. She pointed to a bunch of dolls lined in a row against the wall. "I call them my children." I don't know how I knew, but I knew for sure Shirley Quails was crazy when she called those dolls her *children*. I didn't let on because I knew enough to know crazy people do crazy things.

"They're very nice," I said. "But I have to go now." I didn't wait for her to answer. I ran down the stairs and out the front door. I got my bicycle and pedaled as fast as I could with the wind to my back pushing me along. I never looked behind me in case crazy Shirley was following me with her crazy dolls all riding bicycles. I pedaled and pedaled and was home in no time, my heart beating like it would jump out of my chest. I threw myself into the safety of Momma's arms.

"When are we moving back to Mackinac Island?" I asked. "Crazy people live on this road. I don't think I'm going to like it here."

"Give it time," Momma said. "School will start soon. You'll get to know all the kids, and you'll soon become friends."

"Never," I said. "I'll never be friends with Shirley or anyone else who doesn't love horses."

Chapter 4 – Kittens in the Manger

"One potato, two potato, three potato, four...."

Shirley and I repeat the nonsense rhyme as we walk down our dusty road. She's helping me get the cows for their second milking. It's fun walking and singing silly rhymes. Mr. Quails brought her over when he came to our place to borrow a tractor belt from Papa. Sometimes Shirley doesn't talk much. She usually stays in her house, plays with her dolls, and reads all the *Nancy Drew* books she can find. I lend her some of mine because I like to read them too.

"It's awful hot," I say as I rub sweat beads off my forehead.

"Yes, Katie," Shirley agrees. "I'm hot, too." She loosens the drawstring on her Dale Evans cowgirl hat, and it dangles down her back.

"Do you want to spend the night at my house?" I ask. She doesn't say anything for a minute, but then nods her head. "We'll have lots of fun. We can play with my dolls or read or climb the ladder to the haymow and color in my new Lassie coloring book. Maybe Mama will make us popcorn."

Again, Shirley doesn't talk. We're at the gate now, and the cows are waiting for us. They know when it's time to head for the barn. Silver's the lead cow so she wears the bell. I open the gate, and she leads the others out. They march in line and kick up dust as they walk towards the next pasture. Mama always makes us carry switches, but we don't need them. The cows know the way back as well as we do and can find the barn without any help except they can't open the gates. These are milk cows. We call them Maude, Tulip, Goldie, Arbutus, Blanche, and Maggie. We don't have far to walk to the other pasture.

Once the cows are in the field leading to the barn, I close the gate and we walk on the road again. I ask Shirley if she wants to look in a rotten fencepost to see a bird's nest. She agrees. I pick up a stone and throw it at my favorite post. A bird flies out. We throw down our switches and grab the post with both hands. Then we balance on the bottom string of barbed wire and look for the nest. Our heads bang together as we sneak a peek.

There isn't much light, but if we squint we can see four tiny flesh-colored birds waiting to be fed. Their mouths are open, but their eyes are closed. They have no feathers on their skinny bodies. They make peeping sounds. I want to stick my hand into the nest, but I know if I disturb them, the mother won't return and the babies will die. Shirley asks if there are other posts with baby birds, but I say no because I've been looking in all of them and haven't found anything.

We jump the ditch and run the rest of the way down the road until we reach my porch. Shirley's dad is still visiting with Papa so we ask if she can spend the night. He says yes. Then Mr. Quails and Squeaky, Shirley's twin brother, say goodbye, get in their truck, and drive down our lane leaving a tunnel of dust behind them.

After supper Mama tells us we can play. We don't have to help wash the dishes. I grab Shirley's hand, and we head for the haymow. After we climb the ladder, I reach for my satchel and take out two coloring books and a box of crayons. We start coloring. We're quiet a long time, and then Shirley asks if I want to hear what happened yesterday. I'm surprised because she almost never talks about herself or her family. Squeaky's just the opposite. He talks all the time.

"Sure," I say. "What happened?"

"Katie, it's a long story."

"We have lots of time. It won't get dark for hours yet." I don't think her story will be very interesting so I continue coloring a picture of Lassie pulling Timmy out of the swimming hole.

"Yesterday Mom needed eggs for a cake she was baking. We didn't have any in the fridge so she sent me to the barn to get some. We have lots of chickens, but I forgot to check for eggs in the morning. The first place I looked was in the barn where one of our hens has a nest in an empty manger. The barn was quiet except for Fuzzy, our oldest cat. She was making an awful noise."

"Why?" I ask. Her story is better than I thought. I put down my crayon.

"I'm coming to that," Shirley says. "Fuzzy jumped in the manger and went underneath the oat box. I stuck my hand in to pet her, but instead of feeling her warm body, I felt something small and cold and lifeless. My fingers wrapped around it, and I knew I was holding a dead kitten. I found three more. They were gray and white."

"Are you kidding?" I ask. "Who would put dead kittens in a manger? Are you making this up?"

"No, it's the truth. Just listen. I ran to the house and told Mom what I had found, and we ran back to the barn. Fuzzy had taken the kittens out of the manger and laid them in the sunlight. I started crying."

"I would have cried, too. What happened next?"

"Mom told me to go back to the house and get a shoebox and some tissue paper while she got a shovel. I wrapped each kitten in the soft red paper left over from Christmas. Fuzzy cried as Mom and I buried her babies in the pet cemetery behind the barn. That's where they are now. We bury everything in that cemetery. Even the mice that get caught in traps."

Shirley starts crying, and I cry with her. I've never buried a mouse, but I've helped bury lots of animals, and I always cry. Everybody thinks I'm sassy and sometimes I am, but I have feelings, too. I ask Shirley if she sang a hymn. She said they sang what they remembered of the "Battle Hymn of the Republic" which I don't think is a real hymn, but she says it's better than most. We go to different churches so maybe she's right. When we stop crying, we continue coloring. We're quiet for a long time. Then Shirley asks a strange question.

"Do you ever feel like jumping in the river and not bobbing to the top but sinking to the bottom? Do you ever feel like just floating away?" I tell her I never think of such a thing. I ask why she does. "I don't know," she says. "Strange things just pop into my head for no reason at all."

Soon dusk falls and Mama calls us in. I'm glad it's time for bed. I hope I don't hear another story about dead kittens or sinking to the bottom of the river. I give Shirley a pair of my shortie pajamas. We don't say much as we fall asleep, but all night long I dream about four gray kittens. They're not wrapped in soft Christmas paper and nestled in a pretty shoebox. They're crying by the riverbank. Their little paws are reaching out, trying to save Shirley as she quietly sinks farther and farther into the cold, dark water of the Waishkey River down the road from my house.

Chapter 5 – Cross-Eyed Boy

I'm Flint Flanders and everybody says I can't steer clear of trouble. I guess they're right because today was the second day of school, and I landed in the principal's office all because of a girl. Candy Shirtz stole my heart last year in fifth grade. Although she lives just down the road, I hadn't seen her all summer.

As soon as school was over in May, Ma farmed me out to the relatives in Pickford who needed help with haying and other farm chores. I'm a good worker and earned enough money to buy two new sets of school clothes, one pair of white Keds, a blue three-ring notebook, a dozen No. 2 yellow pencils, a small *Webster's Pocket Dictionary*, and a plastic protractor. I don't know how to use a protractor, but I liked the name of it. The saleslady said I was a planner. I didn't know what that was, but the lady said it in a friendly voice so I guessed it was something good.

The day started out fine. I woke up early and washed in cold water and dried myself on a rough towel made from a chicken feed sack. It's a good towel. I'm going to make a feed sack towel for Candy as a Christmas present if my lazy twin sisters don't steal my idea. I dressed in a hurry, but took time combing my blonde hair. Ma always chopped it off when school got out for the summer, but this time I fooled her. I let my hair grow and wore a cap. When I came home last week, she never even noticed how long it was.

I had all my school stuff ready to go and took one last look in the mirror. Even with eyes that cross, I sure look good. My white tee shirt's tucked into my Levi's. My belt's real leather and one of a kind. Before Pops ran off last year, he went to the fair at Kinross and asked the man at the leather booth to stamp my name on it. The man got the letters mixed up and spelled my name wrong. He spelled it "Flnit," but I don't care. I'm the only kid in school who has a belt with his name on it. If anybody laughs at the spelling, I stick my fingers in their eyes, and they don't laugh again.

Ma, Jazz, and Jill were still asleep when I left, and the house was quiet. I said goodbye like I always do. I got a habit of talking to things that ain't real. That's just my way. I said howdy to the birds as I walked down our lane and waited for the bus. My road's the last one so I knew it would be full, and I'd have to sit with Blew and Johnny. They're my pals. Sometimes Candy sits with Shirley and Katie in front of me.

Finally the bus roared to a stop. I was right. It was packed. "Shove over," I said to Johnny, and he shoved over onto Blew's lap. Blew shoved him back. I almost fell off the seat. I punched Johnny. He squealed like a pig dumped in boiling water. Mean Gene, the bus driver, yelled, "You boys settle down back there or I'll stop the bus and you can walk the rest of the way." We settled down. When Candy got on, she walked past me without saying a word.

Recess is when the real trouble started. Squeaky likes Candy as much as I do. She still hadn't said hello to me or said one word about my long hair, but she smiled at Squeaky and talked to him. I'll never believe she likes him more than me. At recess it was easy to grab the basketball from him and throw it to the fourth graders who have recess at the same time. Squeaky got mad and chased me. I shinnied up the flagpole.

"Here, suey," I yelled and took a stone from my pocket and flung it at him. At the same time I released the stone, I also released my hold on the pole and down I went. Then I grabbed some muddy stones and slung them at Squeaky who slung them back and called me a "cross-eyed beggar." The fight was on. It didn't last long because the playground aide grabbed us by our ears and dragged us to the principal's office right next to our classroom. Everyone heard the paddle as it landed on our bottoms. Whack! Whack! Whack! Principal Jackson asked why we couldn't get through the second day of school without fighting. He told us to leave immediately and walk home.

We went back to class. Everybody stared at us as we got our jackets. Miss Penny, our English teacher, said we were naughty boys and had acted in a very immature way. Didn't we know we were in the sixth grade now, she asked, and didn't we know we shouldn't fight on the playground or any other place? She harped on and on until we hurried out the door.

"See what you've done," I said as we started walking.

"Me? You started it," Squeaky said. "You wanted to impress Candy. You're the idiot."

"I ain't no idiot. You are."

"Shut up," Squeaky said.

"Shut up yourself." We walked two miles and snapped at each other like hungry turtles before we settled on a shaky truce and swapped slingshots. I told Squeaky Candy belonged to me. Squeaky said she was his, and he'd fight every day for her before he'd see her go off with a cross-eyed idiot. I laughed and said cross-eyed or not, I planned to marry her. Squeaky said Candy would never marry a good-for-nothing Flanders who had nothing in his pockets but holes.

"She'll marry me before she marries you," I said. Then I punched him. He stayed down but yelled that Candy would marry him before she'd hitch herself to me. I stared at him and raised my right eyebrow which made my eyes look scary. Then I laughed. I used the slingshot to fire a stone at a crow that was minding its own business eating a dead porcupine by the side of the ditch.

"We'll see who Candy marries," Squeaky yelled. "We'll see." I bet he watched me walk down the road. He always said I had a swagger that made me look like I had the world by the tail. We're both dirt poor, but Squeaky knows that I know that Candy is mine. I whistled all the way home. My new clothes were filthy. Luckily I bought two tee shirts. The other one's black so it won't show the dirt, not too much anyway. Before I went to bed, Ma gave me a good thrashing and cut off all my hair. I'm proud of her. I'm Pop's son, and it ain't easy raising me.

I dreamed of Candy all night. When I got up this morning, the house was quiet, and the cat was meowing for her breakfast. I put some Shredded Wheat and cream in her dish, and then I did some thinking. I've got to do better if I'm going to make it through this year. As soon as I get to school, I'll apologize to the principal. I won't mean it, of course, but it's the manly thing to do. Then I'll apologize to Candy for getting in a fight and that I will mean. She won't talk to me on the bus so I'll wait until the girls jump rope at recess and then I'll join them. When she turns the rope, I'll get close enough to whisper in her ear. I hope she don't slug me. Once I had a plan, I got going. No point in wearing my cap. Now I look like all the other country boys. Boys in town got it easy. They can grow their hair long because they never get lice.

I whistled as I walked down the lane. If I don't flunk any more grades, I've got seven years ahead of me before I'm a free man. Maybe I'll marry Candy after graduation, or maybe I'll enlist in the Army. Pops always said gals like a feller in a uniform. When my time with Uncle Sam is up, I'll come home and marry Candy if Squeaky ain't beat me to it. Then we'll move to Detroit, and I'll get a job on the line at a Chevy factory. Or maybe Pops will come back with two A&P bags overflowing with money, and we'll be rich. Then Candy will marry me for sure, and I won't have to join the Army. Maybe Ma will get religion and sober up and be the Ma I always wanted. Maybe some dimwitted hicks will come along and marry my lazy sisters. Maybe my eyes will uncross.

I whistled louder. Today's gonna be a good day because life is full of possibilities when you're a planner.

Chapter 6 – The Cold War and Bones

Today our history teacher, Mrs. Hubbard, told us October 4, 1957, is a very sad day because the Russians launched their Sputnik and beat the Americans into space. "You'll never forget this day," she yelled as she hit the blackboard with her ruler. "It's a day of shame for America. Imagine, beaten by the Reds. It's unthinkable! Bow your heads and pray God's blessing on our inept leaders." When we finished praying for inept leaders, whatever that means, Mrs. Hubbard told us to open our Weekly Reader and get to work.

I leaned over and asked Larry Lawson what a Sputnik was. "Katie," he said. "It's some kind of new doughnut the Russians 'dunked' not 'launched.' Mrs. Hubbard got her facts wrong again." Then he giggled. I didn't know whether to believe him or the teacher. Sometimes she does get mixed up.

Mrs. Hubbard is always harping about the Cold War. She's afraid there's going to be a nuclear war. Once a week she makes us practice saving ourselves by hiding underneath the art table. There's only room for four kids so we take turns being saved. Mrs. Hubbard hides in the broom closet and takes one kid with her. Nobody wants to go in the closet because she has a gas problem if you know what I mean. The rest of us squeeze underneath our desk which is easy to do if the desk is new, but impossible if it's old because there's no room. Today Mrs. Hubbard yapped on and on about the Dawn of the Space Age and the Arms Race and Radioactive Fallout and the Lack of Space Commitment on the part of President Eisenhower. Near the end of class, I raised my hand.

"Mrs. Hubbard," I said. "Can I ask a question?"

"Katie, don't you mean 'may' you ask a question," she corrected. "Yes, you may if you're quick about it." She collected our papers and put them in a neat stack at the end of her desk. Her hair had gone limp. Long white strands hung around her shoulders like broken strings on a fiddle. Her red marking pencil was jabbed behind her ear like it always is.

"If you believe in God, why are you so worried about the Cold War?" I asked. Kids snickered. Mrs. Hubbard stared at me. Her face got all wrinkled and instead of yelling at me like I expected, she began to cry.

"I don't know," she said. Her voice sounded like Mama's when she's all worn out from a hard day's work. I felt bad.

"Gee, I'm sorry," I mumbled, but Mrs. Hubbard didn't answer. She just cried louder and left the room. Larry patted my hand.

"You did good," he whispered. "You did real good."

But I didn't think so. I promised myself I'd be nice to Mrs. Hubbard so she won't fail me for making her cry. Then it was time for science class, and I forgot all about her. Today Mr. Prichard is going to talk about cutting up a frog. We're too young to do that, but he's weird and wants us to know what to expect so when the time comes we'll be ready. As if we're going to remember anything he says three years from now when we're in the ninth grade.

Bones hangs in a corner of Mr. Prichard's room. I hate that skeleton, standing there grinning his stupid horse-like grin, reminding me of what I look like underneath my skin. Bones gives me the creeps. I sit in the front row, and Bones is directly to my left. I see him every time I look at Mr. Prichard. I don't know if the other kids notice, but Bones has a way of slowly moving from side to side whenever Mr. Prichard opens the window to let in fresh air. He starts talking about cutting open a frog and taking out its innards. I watch old Bones sway in the breeze, and it takes my mind off the disgusting stuff I'm supposed to be remembering.

"...slice it open and separate all the internal organs. Then pull out its intestines and make sure you get all of them. Then...."

My mind floats away as I look at the empty head of Bones, at where his brain would be if he had one. Then I look for his stomach, but I'm not sure where it is. There are lots of holes in his frame. I figure his intestines must spill out of some of them. In my mind's eye, I see the long sausages that hold our manure in place until we get the urge to push it out. I imagine Bones sitting on the pot getting rid of his supper and without realizing it, I laugh.

"Kathleen Clark, I'm glad you find this amusing." Mr. Prichard's voice is stern. His eyes glare into mine. I feel my face flame red. I know he's mad at me when he calls me Kathleen instead of Katie.

"Sorry, Sir," I say.

"Tell the class what you found so amusing."

"Nothing."

"Nothing made you laugh?"

"It's Bones, Sir."

"Bones?"

"Yes. He moves behind you."

"What do you mean 'he moves'?" Mr. Prichard turns and looks at Bones who, of course, is not moving. "Class, how many of you saw Bones move?" He asks the question in such a way that anyone who might want to agree with me wouldn't dare. He leans forward and stares at us. "Well, who other than Kathleen saw Bones move? Answer me." His eyes roam the room. No one, not Flint, Blew, Larry, or even Johnny who likes me say a word. They're all chickens.

"No, I didn't think so," Mr. Prichard says. "Kathleen, you will stay after class when the bell rings." He continues to lecture. "As I was saying, it's best to be prepared. Doesn't Mrs. Hubbard prepare you for a Russian attack? Of course she does, the same as I'm preparing you for science class when you're older. If only you youngsters paid attention, you might learn something and not have to repeat grades." The bell rings before he says anything more. Everyone flies out the door as if the room was on fire. Mr. Prichard turns to me.

"Well, what have you got to say for yourself?" He crosses his arms on his chest. Bones moves behind him.

"Nothing, Sir." Bones sways.

"Why are you smiling?"

"I'm not, Sir." Bones sways again.

"Why are you laughing?"

"I'm not, Sir." Bones' long fingers flutter as the wind blows through the open window. My body is shaking from invisible laughter bubbling inside of me.

"I'm going to call your parents and inform them of your rude behavior."

"We don't have a phone," I lie.

"Then I'll write a note. Make sure you give it to your mother." He scribbles something on a piece of paper, folds it, and hands it to me. As I take it, a gust of wind rocks Bones. I laugh out loud. Mr. Prichard doesn't explode or say a word. He turns and looks at Bones whose whole body is flapping like sheets on a clothesline. Mr. Prichard grabs the note from my hand and tells me to leave the room.

Next day when I get to class, Bones is away from the window. He's in a far corner at the back of the room. As much as I hate that skeleton, I miss him, too. There isn't anything to look at except bald old Mr. Prichard who weighs at least 200 pounds and drips sweat from his enormous ears. Sometimes I chuckle to myself, but I'm careful not to laugh. When Mr. Prichard asks why I'm chuckling, I lie and say I'm clearing my throat. Then he moves on to the next kid and leaves me alone.

I hope Mr. Prichard dies on a day when our country finally beats the Russians into space so nobody will pay any attention to him. I hope he doesn't get much of a send-off. I hope everyone is glued to their television sets. I hope some undertaker donates his body to medical scientists and when they finish with him, they pass his skeleton along to some poor public school just like Brimley's. Mr. Prichard might hang in a science lab, sway in the breeze, and get another kid in trouble. I snicker at the thought.

"Kathleen," Mr. Prichard yells. "Will you please tell the class what's so funny?"

"Nothing, Sir," I say. "Nothing at all."

Chapter 7 – Daisy's Unread Story

Nobody wanted to hear my story. I wrote it today when Miss Penny said we had to write a paper about a famous person. Most of the kids read what they had written, and the kids who were afraid to read got off easy. Miss Penny read for them. I raised my hand, but she didn't call on me. She was standing at the front of the room and my seat is at the back. I thought maybe she couldn't see me so I stood up to get her attention.

"Sit down, Daisy," she said. "Wait your turn." But my turn never came. English class ended and everyone went to lunch. I hung around her desk and asked if I could read my work after lunch. She said no, it would eat into our spelling time. Then I asked if she would like to hear my story while she ate her sandwich, but she said, no, she was reading the newspaper and didn't want to be disturbed. I shoved the story back in my desk, picked up my lunch pail, and went to the lunchroom to join the other kids.

"Miss Penny won't let me read my story," I said as they made room for me at the table. Blew and Squeaky stuck up for me. "That's too bad. Read it to us," but when I told them I left it in my desk, they didn't say *go get it* so I knew they didn't want to hear it, either. Candy and Elizabeth said they'd like to hear it, but they had other things to do before the bell rang. They ran after the boys.

When they were gone, I sat alone and looked at myself in my shiny silver metal thermos cup. I don't look too bad. My hair is clean and my bangs are even across my forehead. Most of my teeth are straight, and my fingernails are short and clean. I don't smell of barn like some kids do. I don't know why Miss Penny doesn't like me unless it's because I have a club foot and limp when I walk.

Lunchtime was almost over. Mr. Straw smiled at me as he swept up the mess on the floor. I asked him if he wanted to hear my story and he said, "Maybe later, I'm busy now." I knew that was his way of saying *no*. Then I asked his wife, the cook, and she said, "I'm up to my elbows in dishwater. Maybe at second recess," but I can't come into the kitchen then which meant she didn't want to hear it either.

I walked back to my room, sat at my desk, and took out my story. I reread it and made a few corrections. Then I folded it into a fan and used it to move the air around me. Through closed eyes, I pictured my classroom. It's small and painted green. My desk is next to the window. Sometimes I daydream when I'm supposed to be working. My mind wanders. Sometimes it flies off with a seagull and travels Lake Superior, following the freighters as they sail on the Great Lakes. Right now my mind was wandering through my story. I never knew I could write one so special.

The bell rang and kids piled back into the room. Before spelling, we took a test on nouns, pronouns, and verbs. After the test, I asked Miss Penny if I could read my story. She reminded me we have a spelling test now and asked why I thought my story was special. I told her I thought the kids would like it because it's about someone famous we all know and it's funny.

"What famous person ever came to Brimley?" she asked.

"If I tell you, it'll spoil the surprise." Miss Penny drummed her fingers on the pile of papers on her desk.

"Give me that story, Daisy," she said. I handed it to her.

"You made it into a fan. It's all wrinkled and smudged. You'll have to rewrite it if you want to read it."

"But the words are the same even if the paper is a mess."

The room got very quiet. "You are rude," Miss Penny said. She wadded my story into a ball and threw it in the wastepaper basket. I stared at it. "Dig it out if you want to," she said and turning away she explained the importance of knowing that a noun is not a person, place, or thing. It's the *name* of a person, place, or thing. Then she told us to get out a piece of paper for our spelling test.

I reached into the basket and my fingers curled around the little hard ball of paper. My story was about God. I wrote that God got scared when Eve ate the apple and gave some to Adam because He didn't expect them to be disobedient. It wasn't in His master plan so He quickly made up a new plan to show everything He created that He was still the boss and had to be obeyed. I said that God looked like Jackie Gleason when he gets mad at his wife and threatens to send her to the moon.

In my story, the animals joined Adam and Eve and voted to send God to the moon because He was the big cheese and that's where He belonged. I felt guilty when I was writing it because Father Gray says we're not supposed to mock God, but my story came so fast, I thought maybe it was God who put the idea into my head. But nobody will ever hear what I wrote. As soon as I get home, I'm feeding it to the pigs.

I limped back to my desk. If I ever get another creative thought, I'll ignore it and write about something safe like cattails or shipwrecks or how people make a living in Bay Mills. I stared out the window and pretended I was sailing on the *Edward L. Ryerson*, the most beautiful freighter on the Great Lakes. I pretended Miss Penny was the captain and the crew mutinied, and we threw her overboard. She sank like a stone to the bottom of the lake, and on icy cold nights her ghost could be seen splashing through the choppy water. She's holding a sharp pencil in her bony hand. She's threatening to jab little kids, but she doesn't scare anybody because her ghost is blind. The children laugh and run away as she chases after them.

A smile spread across my lips as I wrote down our spelling words. Maybe this writing business isn't so bad after all. Maybe I'll become a famous writer and tell stories about Miss Penny and all the other teachers who made a kid's life in school miserable, especially the kids who were too fat, too skinny, too poor, too dumb, smelled like barn, or had a crooked foot. I can't wait to go home and get started.

Chapter 8 – A Trip to Castle Rock

"Well, Daisy, it looks like you'll get to see Castle Rock today. How big do you think the castle is?"

"As tall as a mountain, I guess. What do you think, Blew?"

"Well, I bet it's taller than Point Iroquois Lighthouse, but I don't think it's as tall as a mountain. There ain't no mountains in Brimley or the Soo, and there sure ain't none on our road so I guess there ain't none in St. Ignace."

"Don't you guys know anything? Castle Rock isn't a castle. It's a big rock carved out of the hillside with steps leading up to it."

"If you're so smart, Elizabeth, why do they call it a castle?"

"I'm smart, Blew, because I read. The Indians built it over a thousand years ago. They liked the word 'castle' so that's what they called it."

"You're nuts, Elizabeth. Them Indians built teepees. Everyone knows soldiers built forts and kings built castles. You ain't as smart as you think you are."

"You're both wrong," Flint says. "It was them fur traders who built the fort and the castle, and it wasn't no thousand years ago. It was a hundred years ago, so there."

"Ah, what'd you know, Flint? You flunked kindergarten."

"You better shut your mouth, Blew, or I'll shut it for you."

"You're all wrong," Katie corrects us. "It was the widows who built the fort to keep out the cougars and wolves and moose. After all the men were killed, it was up to the widows to defend themselves and their babies. If it wasn't for them, there wouldn't even be a Castle Rock. They're the ones who made it."

"Ah, shut up, Katie. You don't know nothing about nothing," Flint says.

"Flint, I bet she knows more than you do," I say.

"Blew, you wanna fight?" Flint asks.

"You bet I do."

"Settle down back there, boys, or I'll turn this bus around and head back to the school," Mean Gene yells.

"Mr. Gene is right," Mrs. Lark, our homeroom teacher, says. "Stop fighting. None of you know the history of Castle Rock or Fort Michilimackinac because you don't pay attention in your classes. I'll tell you the true story if you promise to be quiet and listen." Everybody nods. It was Mrs. Lark's idea to have the field trip today so we better be quiet, or we'll land back in the classroom.

"It's like this," Mrs. Lark begins. "Many years ago Frenchmen came to our country when they heard about all the wild animals that could be trapped. Beavers were especially sought after because their pelts were made into top hats for gentlemen. Minks were important for their pelts that were made into fur coats for rich ladies. To protect themselves from Odawa Indians, the French built a garrison that came to be known as Fort Michilimackinac."

"What's a garrison," Johnny asks.

"You shouldn't interrupt," Mrs. Lark says. "But I'll answer your question. A garrison is a military outpost. It's made up of buildings surrounded by walls."

"Were the French afraid of the Indians?" Larry inquires.

"I suppose so," Mrs. Lark says. "There were no Indians in France."

"I'm an Indian," Larry says. "Ain't nobody afraid of me."

"That's different," Mrs. Lark remarks. "You're a Chippewa Indian. Now, let me continue."

"Did the French kill all the Indians and steal their corn?" Squeaky asks.

"Did the French eat the Indians?" Flint wants to know.

"How'd they catch the beavers and how many minks did they trap and how did they fish without nets?" Larry asks more questions.

"Children, you're very inquisitive. You'll have to check out books at the library in Sault Ste. Marie and learn all about the French and Indians who lived in our area in the 1700s. We're almost at Castle Rock. Make sure you bring your lunch with you. We'll eat at one of the tables after we climb down from the Rock.

You'll have time to go to the Trading Post and buy a souvenir if you brought money. If not, just look at all the different items."

"Hey, Blew. I bet she don't know anymore about the castle or the fort than we do," Johnny whispers to me. "She's as dumb as we are. Whoever heard of a hat made out of a beaver pelt?"

"Right," I say. "We tripped her up with all our questions."

"Here we are," Mean Gene announces. "Everybody out."

"Single file," Mrs. Lark says. "And no talking." There are 25 kids. We make a long line and start marching towards the castle steps, but the first kid stops and everybody behind him falls like dominoes. "Hey, look over there," Russell Prats yells. "That's Paul Bunyan and his blue ox." Nobody likes Russell because Mrs. Lark always chooses him to lead the line, but we're not mad at him now because we see Paul Bunyan and Babe. They're as big as giants. I can't believe it. There really was a man who owned a blue ox.

"Tell us the story of Paul Bunyan and his ox," I yell.

"Not now, Blew," Mrs. Lark says. "Maybe while we're eating lunch. Be careful on the steps. I don't want anyone falling or twisting an ankle. And definitely no running. Daisy, take my hand. If you can't climb all the way, sit down and wait for us."

"I can do it. I'll just go slow. I don't need your hand."

"We might as well be old women," Flint whispers to me. "At this rate, it'll take forever to climb all the way to the top."

"Yeah, but look at the girls ahead of us. We might get to see underneath their dresses the higher they go and the lower we are."

"Great idea, Blew. Let's walk slower."

"Shake a leg, you guys," Larry says until we tell him our plan. He agrees and before we know it all the boys are lagging behind. Mrs. Lark is almost to the top when she turns around and sees us huddled together. "Keep walking, boys," she hollers. "And keep your eyes focused on where you're stepping, not on what's ahead of you. If I see any of you gawking around again, you're all going back to the bus. Understand?"

"Yes, Mrs. Lark."

"I didn't hear you. Your heads were pointed down. Look up when you answer me."

"But you told us to look at the steps," Flint yells.

"Never mind," she says and shakes her head. We continue walking and peeking at the girls until we reach the top. Wow, what a disappointment. It wasn't worth climbing all those steps, and we didn't even get to see the girls' underwear. Now all we see are millions of trees and lots of rocks, but none as big as the one we're on and it ain't a castle. It's just a chunk of stone that sticks out farther than the rest. Big deal. We can see Lake Huron, though, so I guess that's something.

"Take your time, children, and survey your surroundings," Mrs. Lark instructs us.

"We see this every day at home," Daisy complains. "I thought we were going to visit a real castle with a drawbridge and horses and men in silver armor. This is just trees and rocks. It's not a castle at all. It wasn't worth the trouble."

"Look at the beauty all around you, Daisy," Mrs. Lark exclaims. "We've very fortunate to live in the Upper Peninsula. People in cities do not have the opportunity to see such splendor."

"People in cities don't have a club foot, either."

"I'll carry you down," Johnny offers.

"Me, too," Squeaky volunteers.

"I'll do the carrying because I'm the strongest." Larry speaks in a loud voice.

"That's very nice of you boys," Mrs. Lark says. "But nobody will carry Daisy. She'll walk beside me. Class, take one last look and remember what you see. Tomorrow Miss Penny will ask you to write a report about our field trip."

After we eat, we go to the Trading Post. Flint tells Russell he has 25 cents to spend. He wants to buy something special for Candy. I think it's stupid to waste money on a girl. I'm gonna buy myself a tomahawk.

"What's your favorite thing here?" Flint asks Candy.

"I like everything, especially the Indian headdress. What do you like, Flint?"

"I like the headdress, too, but I think that beaded bracelet is pretty."

"That's for a girl," Candy says.

"I know," Flint agrees.

"Are you going to buy it for your mother?"

"No."

"It would be nice if you bought it for her."

"Then maybe I will, Candy, if you think it's a good idea."

"Well, it is a little small."

"It might fit you," Flint sounds hopeful.

"It might."

"Want to try it on?"

"Maybe."

"Hey, Candy," Squeaky yells. "Look at what I bought for you." He holds up a headdress covered in feathers and beads. Candy runs over to him.

"I love it," she says. Squeaky smiles at her. Then he looks at Flint and laughs.

"Hey, Flint," I yell. "Take a look at this miniature jackknife. It's only a quarter."

"Good idea, Blew. I'll buy it for myself."

"Hurry and make your purchases," Mrs. Lark orders. "It's time to go. Those of you who already bought your gifts, get back on the bus. Sit in the same seat you were sitting in on the ride here. If you bought candy or gum, you'll have to wait until you get home before eating or chewing it. Those are the rules, as you well know."

On the ride back to school, everyone's quiet. Flint sits next to me. He's mad at Squeaky.

"Blew," he says. "I bet Squeaky stole his mother's egg money. He never has more than a nickel in his pocket. Candy ain't my gal anymore if an Indian headdress can win her over. At least she ain't my gal today."

"Gals is like that," I say. "You can't trust 'em."

"You're right. I should know that by now."

"Hey, Flint, how come you're so quiet?" Squeaky yells.

"I was thinking about that blue ox." Flint shakes his fist at Squeaky.

"Settle down back there," Mean Gene yells. "Or I'll head for the jailhouse instead of the school."

"Might as well be the same," I say.

"You got that right," Flint says. "For sure, Blew, you got that right."

Chapter 9 – Shirley's Piano

"That was a wild rainstorm we had yesterday. Were you scared, Shirley?"

"No, Katie. Not until Mom lit the kerosene lamp, and our faces looked like monsters."

"I know what you mean. When the lights went out and Mama lit ours, we all looked scary. First it was funny, but when the oak tree crashed to the ground, nothing was funny anymore. It was a miracle it didn't fall on our house. Show me your new piano."

"It's not new. It's an old upright Pap bought at the auction in Pickford. He's always buying something. Once he bought a fancy wristwatch for Mom, but she never wore it so he gave it away. Another time he bought a stack of 78 rpm records for our Victrola and a box full of sheet music. C'mon. The piano's in the front room."

"I like this room," I say. "The wallpaper with pink roses is pretty. I like that picture, too. Is the beautiful lady your relative?"

"I don't know. She might be," Shirley says. "Everybody likes this room except Mom. She's afraid of it. In the old days, it's where they laid out dead people. Mom's parents were waked in this room. Once she said she saw a ghost that looked like her mother, but I'm not afraid. Does the room scare you?"

"No, I don't believe in ghosts, at least I don't think I do. In our church we pray to the Holy Ghost so I guess ghosts are good things. What will you play on the piano?"

"I don't know how to play anything yet, but I'm trying to teach myself. Let's bang on the keys and make something that sounds like music."

"Where's the sheet music your Pap bought? Maybe we can figure it out."

"Mom burned it in the woodstove. The notes wouldn't mean anything to us because we can't read them. I'll take the left keys. You take the ones to the right."

"Okay. Let's make as much noise as the storm." We pound on the keys, trying to make them sound like thunder. Shirley's Mom runs into the room.

"Close the lid," she commands. "I can't stand the noise, and I don't want you two in here alone. Come into the kitchen." We close the lid and follow her. Suddenly, the sky gets dark, the wind begins to roar, and rain pounds on the roof. Mrs. Quails starts praying. I don't know why but giggles come to my throat. I try to swallow them down without much luck. Shirley shoots me a warning look. I know it isn't funny, but we must look silly as we huddle together. In a few minutes, the rain stops and the wind dies down, but thunder booms. I jump to my feet as I hear a loud crash.

"Can I look outside and see what fell?" I ask.

"No, Katie, of course not." Mrs. Quails' voice is stern. The lights dim, then go out. The kitchen is plunged into darkness. I reach for Shirley's hand but can't find it. Instead, I feel something cold as ice next to me. The lights flicker and come back on.

"What was that cold thing I felt?" I ask. Shirley looks at her mother.

"Just wind from the open windows," she says. "I forgot to close them." She walks over to the windows, but none are open.

"You touched my hand," Squeaky says, but he doesn't sound very convincing. "It's always cold as ice. Feel." He sticks out his hand, but I don't want to touch it. "Go ahead," he says, but I won't. Then I hear someone playing the piano. The sound is beautiful.

"That's Mom," Shirley explains. "She knows how to play chords, but she won't teach me. She says I have to learn on my own just like she did." We go back to the piano room. Mrs. Quails looks beautiful. Her blonde hair is long, and she has a pink rose stuck in it. She must have taken it from the vase on top of the piano. She doesn't see us because her eyes are closed. She runs her fingers over the keys like they're old friends. I don't know the name of the song, but I've never heard anything like it. It's different from church music or what the man on the radio plays. I don't want it to stop. I want it to go on and on because it's the most beautiful music I've ever heard.

"Your mother's beautiful," I tell Shirley. "So is her music." Shirley smiles, but when Mrs. Quails hears my voice, she slams down the piano lid and turns to me.

"Go home," she says. "You spoiled everything."

"Gee, Mrs. Quails, I'm sorry. I didn't mean to upset you. The music was beautiful."

"Just go home," she repeats.

I grab my jacket. I don't want to admit it, but this house gives me the creeps. Elizabeth said it was spooky, but I didn't believe her. Maybe she was right. Shirley walks me to the door.

"I'm sorry, Katie" she apologizes. "One day I'll tell you why Mom is the way she is. Please don't tell anyone at school that she's mixed up. Please."

"Don't worry," I say. "I won't tell anyone." I get my bike and pedal home as fast as I can. Lightning flashes and thunder booms. I pedal faster. There's something weird going on in that house. I don't know what it is, but I think Shirley's grandmother touched my hand. The fingers were bony as well as cold. A shudder runs down my back.

Chapter 10 – Pictures in the October Clouds

"Katie. Tell me everythin'. Every little detail," Blew demands.

"No," I say.

"Why not?"

"You should have come with us today."

"I ain't never goin' to no funeral parlor. Maybe to the beer parlor, but you ain't never gonna catch me where dead people are. No funeral parlor. No graveyard."

"And I'm not going to tell you one thing about Granny's funeral."

"Never?"

"Never."

"When will never end?"

"Never will never end. It will go on and on and on. Do you understand?"

Blew thinks for a minute then scratches his head. "Crazy as it sounds, I guess I do. Never's like nothin'."

"Right. Now, are we going bike riding or not?"

"We ain't goin' nowhere. We're gonna stay right here and talk about death." Blew crosses his arms and sits as straight as a totem pole. I look away from him and dangle my legs over the edge of the haymow and look at the clouds. All of a sudden, I see a picture in them that looks like Granny. I nudge Blew.

"Look at that cloud over there. What do you see?" He follows the direction of my finger.

"I don't see nothin' but a cloud."

"It's Granny's face. She's smiling at us." Blew shades his eyes and leans forward.

"I still don't see nothin'."

"Look harder."

"That ain't nothin' but a cloud. You're all mixed up. Let's talk about death. Mix up the letters, and what do you get? THEAD. Is that a word? ADETH. Is that a word? HTAED. Is that a word? HATED. Is that a word? Well, is HATED a word or ain't it?"

"What do you think?"

"Right. That's why people hate to talk about death. They hate it 'cause they're scared of it, but it's only a word. A stupid word like all them other stupid words in our spellin' books."

"You're crazy. Go home."

"I ain't crazy, and I ain't goin' home. GOD. Mix up the letters, and what do you get? DOG, that's what you get. Just a plain old dog. Ain't nothin' special about that. You been prayin' to a dog and wonderin' why your prayers ain't gettin' answered."

"You can't call God a dog."

"God don't care about me or you or Granny or nobody else so why should I care about God?"

"Don't say that. It isn't right."

"Okay, Katie, you win. We'll talk about somethin' else." Blew thinks for a minute then points his finger towards the east. "Where's that crow goin'? Or that wren? What kind of bug did that chicken just scratch outta the dirt? How long is an earthworm? Why is it better to step barefoot into a fresh cowpie than an old crusty one?"

"Shut up."

"No, I mean it, Katie. These are good questions. Why don't people ask about things that matter instead of worryin' about God? When I'm old enough, I'll stuff my stuff into a sack, run away, and never look back. I'll be a sailor and work on the *Joseph L. Block*, the best freighter on the Great Lakes. If anybody brings up that God business, I'll throw 'em overboard." Blew stretches out on the hay and closes his eyes. Within two minutes, he's asleep. I watch his chest move up and down as he breathes. Now I can cry. I didn't want to cry before because I'm not a baby, but now it's okay. Blew won't hear me and even if he does, he won't tell anyone. Granny's wake was yesterday. She was buried today. I'm going to miss her.

Katie thinks I'm sleepin', but I ain't. I'm pretendin'. Granny was my Granny too 'cause Katie and me is cousins. It ain't fair that she's dead, but nothin's fair. I figured that out a long time ago. Behind my closed eyes, I wonder where my eyeballs are. I saw a blind man once. He had milky spots where his eyes should of been. When I asked Mam why he had no eyes, she said his mama musta looked at somethin' bad when he was in her belly and so his mama marked him. I was only seven when Mam told me that, and I didn't know what she meant. Now I know 'cause I'm marked too. I'm adopted.

Katie knows I am, but she don't know how hard it is. I ain't never told her the truth about how I feel—like I don't belong to nobody—kinda like an old left hand glove that ain't got no right to go with it. Mam showed me a picture of my real mamma once. She had yellow hair. I don't trust no gals with yellow hair.

I open my eyes a crack. Looks like Katie's sleepin'. I might as well catch a nap, too. I ain't in no hurry. I got lots of chores waitin' for me when I get home. I close my eyes tight and letters float before them. ADOPTED. Mix it up, and what've you got? PET, TAP, DEAL, TOAD. I ain't no better than a PET TOAD. That's all I am. Words. They ain't nothin' but a bunch of useless letters mixed up to make kids feel bad about themselves. Altogether, words ain't worth a nickel.

Blew thinks I'm sleeping, but I'm not. I'm thinking about Granny. Three days ago when Papa got up to do the chores, he found Granny lying on the kitchen floor looking at the ceiling instead of making breakfast. She left us and never even said goodbye, not even to Grandpa who didn't know she was dead until Papa woke him. The priest said God needed her, but I don't believe that. There must be lots of old dead people God could talk to. He didn't need Granny. She wasn't even sick.

I hope she's in heaven, but she never went to church not even on Christmas or Easter. I asked Mama why not. She said Granny was too old and crippled to do all the kneeling and standing our church demands. I asked if Granny was a heathen. Mama said no, she was just old and God forgave old folks who had aching bones and preferred their warm bed to a cold church. I said if the church wasn't cold would that make a difference. Mama looked at me and shook her head, but she didn't answer my question.

I open my eyes and watch the clouds again, but I don't see any faces in them. They're just clouds, lazy and fat, drifting through the autumn sky. Then Blew opens his eyes. "You gonna stay up here all day or you gonna bike ride with me?" he asks.

"Get my bike out of the shed. I'll race you to the corner." Soon we won't be able to ride our bikes because the road will be full of snow. As I'm climbing down the ladder, Blew yells.

"Hey, look at that cloud over there. I see Granny wavin' and smilin'. You were right, Katie. She was there all along. I just didn't look hard enough."

Chapter 11 – Katie Tells of Halloween Hazards

"Katie, why are you giggling?" Mama asks.

Mrs. Quails, Mama, and Flint share the front seat while Blew, Shirley, Squeaky, and I are squeezed into the back. Squeaky's perched on Blew's lap. Shirley and I are laughing because the boys look ridiculous. I'm dressed like a witch and so is Shirley. Our pointed paper hats are getting crushed because they scrape against the roof of the car. Squeaky's wearing an old dress, a red wig, and a princess mask. He looks like a girl.

Blew's dressed like a pirate. He wrapped an old rag around his head and colored a piece of gauze black. Then he taped it over his left eye to look like a pirate's patch. He cut off part of his mask where the patch is. He can hardly see where he's going. Flint's a bum. He's wearing ripped overalls, a red plaid hunting shirt, a cap with earflaps, and a man's mask. Our mothers are dressed up, too.

Mama's pretending to be a grand lady in a silver wig, a pretty mask, and a fancy centennial dress. Mrs. Quails is a monster dressed in rags and looks like a refugee from Outer Mongolia, wherever that is. Her mask is dangling from her neck. She can't wear it until we stop at a house for Trick or Treat because she can't see where she's going. Even with her mask off, she almost drove into the ditch a few minutes ago. She said she can't see because of the rain. We all know she's not a very good driver but Mama's worse.

Our masks are hot, our faces sweat inside them, and it's impossible to see out of the tiny eyeholes. We're fighting like we do every Halloween. We've been out for an hour. We're wet and crabby but we don't want to go home because our bags aren't full. People have been stingy with everything except apples that probably came from their backyard. We finally crossed the bridge into Brimley. Maybe now we'll get candy bars. Everybody shouts orders.

"Don't stop at Mr. Keller's house," Blew yells. "He'll give us one stick of Black Jack gum."

"Don't stop at Mr. Prichard's," Flint says. "He'll give us frog guts."

"Ma," Squeaky suggests. "Stop at the bar. Maybe the drunks will give us money." Every year we stop at the bar, and nobody has given us as much as one lousy nickel. I don't know why Squeaky thinks we'll get something this year, but his mother parks by the front door. Mrs. Quails puts on her mask, and we pile out of the car. Before we reach the first step, Squeaky trips over the hem of his dress. He falls on his face.

"I ain't wearing this stinkin' dress another minute," he yells. He tries to pull it off, but it gets tangled in his wig. His mother tells him to tuck the hem in his belt which he does. He looks silly. Anyone who looks at his overalls and oxfords will know he's no more a girl than I am a boy. He wants to go back to the car, but Mrs. Quails won't let him. She reminds him stopping at the beer garden was his idea.

It's dark and smoky inside. A couple old men are sitting at the bar. A man and a woman are sitting at a table. Two guys are playing pool. In one corner, Mrs. Lark is pouring beer into a glass. She's sitting with someone who might be her husband, but he's not white. There's a bottle of beer in front of him. While our mothers and the other kids walk up to the bartender, Squeaky grabs my arm.

"C'mon, Katie," he says and leads me towards Mrs. Lark. I'm glad she doesn't know who we are. That's the great thing about masks. We can pretend to be anybody. Squeaky lets go of my arm, shoves his Piggly Wiggly grocery bag under our teacher's nose and yells "Trick or Treat." He tries to make his voice sound like a girl's, but it doesn't. He isn't fooling anyone.

Mrs. Lark looks like she's been caught with her hand in the cookie jar. Squeaky shakes his bag and yells again. She opens her purse and takes out some change. I can't see how many coins she found, but she throws all of them in his bag and tells us to scram. That's what kids say. It's not proper for a teacher. Maybe Mrs. Lark is drunk. Squeaky shakes his bag at the man sitting across

from her, but instead of giving him money, the man reaches in the bag and takes out a Milky Way.

"You can't do that," Squeaky yells in his own voice. "Gimmie that back." He tries to snatch it from the man, but he raises his arm above his head, and Squeaky can't reach it. "Gimmie it or I'll tell everybody in school Mrs. Lark has a boyfriend." As soon as he says this, Mrs. Quails walks over to the table, puts her hand on Squeaky's ear, and marches him to the bar. Nobody says a word until the bartender laughs. Then everybody laughs, and all the drunks give us money. We run for the door.

As soon as we step outside, it starts raining again. Every year it either rains or snows on Halloween. It's dark as pitch, and we can't see where we're going so, of course, I step in a puddle. Now my shoes are soaked. I'm wearing old ones with holes in the toes so my socks are also wet. Flint reaches for a flashlight in his pocket and drops his bag. Before he can pick it up, a dog comes out of nowhere and grabs it. Squeaky tries to chase Rover, but he can't see where the dog ran.

"Never mind," Mama says. "Everyone will share their candy with you when we get home."

"I'll give you all my apples," Blew offers.

"Want a piece of Dubble Bubble?" Shirley asks.

"I'll give you a penny if I have one," Squeaky adds.

I think for a minute then tell Flint he can have my Mars if he promises not to copy off my paper when we have our spelling test. He agrees. I don't believe him because he always copies. I think it's a fair trade though because I don't have any Mars bars, but he doesn't know that. We pile back in the car. Mama says it's time to go home, but we beg to stay out a little longer. Mrs. Quails says if we all agree on where to stop, we can knock on one more door. Nobody says a word. We're thinking of the best place to go.

We don't want to stop at an old person's house because they'll give us raisins or rotten apples. We know we can't go down another dirt road because Mrs. Quails said the ruts were so bad on the last one, the bottom might fall out of the car if she hits another one. We have to stick to the main road, but nobody has their outside light on. They don't anyone to stop, and if we do, their dogs will chase us. Mrs. Quails says we waited too long to decide so we're going home. Mama agrees. "It's past eight o'clock. Don't forget you have school tomorrow."

How could we forget? Everybody groans, but we take off our masks and ask Mrs. Quails to turn on the overhead light so we can count our loot. She won't because she says she can't see where she's going with the light on. I don't know why Mr. Quails lets her drive. She's almost as bad as Mean Gene who gets stuck in the mud or snow at least once a year and somebody has to get the tractor and pull him out.

Squeaky whispers something in Blew's ear, he whispers in mine, and I whisper in Shirley's. We know how we're going to save our candy and fool Flint. Since the car belongs to Mr. Quails, we're going to hide all the good stuff in a pile underneath the front seat. Squeaky will gather it up when he gets home, and we'll divvy it up after school tomorrow. We'll show Flint our bags and tell him he can take whatever he wants. Our mothers won't yell at us for being selfish, and Flint won't know the truth.

As soon as we get to his house Mrs. Quails turns on the dome light, and we give our bags to her so Flint can take a handful. That's the rule. As much as one hand can hold from each bag but no peeking. He sticks his hand in the bags and fills his pockets and cap with wax lips, Squirrels, Necco Wafers, Root Beer Barrels, and suckers. All the stuff we don't want.

"Where's the candy bars?" he demands. We tell him nobody gave out candy bars this year. He says his ma gave each of us a Snickers, and he's pretty sure Mrs. Quails gave us a Milky Way, and he knows for a fact that my mother put a Mounds in each bag. And what about the Mars bar I promised him? We're quiet for a minute then Blew lies and says he's awful sorry but we ate them. Flint says he didn't smell chocolate and he didn't hear us tear off the wrappers, but it's too late for us to argue with him. His ma's standing on the porch waving at us and yelling at him to get in the house before the rain starts again.

As soon as he slams the car door, we laugh. We think we're pretty smart. Our mothers ask what's so funny, but we don't know what to say so we just laugh louder. The next stop is mine. After school tomorrow, we'll ride our bikes to Squeaky's house and collect our loot. When Mama comes to tuck me in, she sits on the edge of my bed and tells me she's very proud of me and the other kids because we shared our treats with Flint.

"He's a good boy," she says. Then she bends down and kisses my forehead. I feel a little guilty until she mentions that Mr. Quails is selling his car in the morning.

"Tomorrow morning?" I ask. I can't believe my ears.

"Yes, first thing. Rust ate big holes underneath the front seat, and Mr. Quails is tired of fixing them. Goodnight, Katie. Sweet dreams."

I lie in the dark and think for a minute. Now I understand why we felt a draft when we hid the candy bars. In my mind's eye, I see Snickers and Milky Ways and Butterfingers and Mounds all being crushed as cars speed down Six Mile Road and grind our candy into the gravel. So much for our plan. I roll on my side and listen to the rain as it hits our roof. Then I pull the covers over my head. Rats. All that trick or treating for nothing but rotten apples, DumDum suckers, and wrinkled old raisins. What a rotten Halloween this has been.

Chapter 12 – King Tut Day

"What special day is today, November 4?" Miss Penny asks.

"King Tut Day," everybody responds. Miss Penny has been drumming special days of the year into our head since school started. She gives us a handout that we have to read. Then we talk about it in class, and she makes us write a report.

"Excellent. I think everyone is doing an outstanding job remembering all the important days in history."

"But this is English class," Elizabeth says. "Why do we have to know what happened in history?"

"Excellent question, Elizabeth. Mrs. Hubbard is teaching you history. I'm teaching you grammar and punctuation and how to write a report. I'm also introducing you to literature. Sometimes we read fiction stories, and sometimes we read about real people."

"Why don't we have a real reading class like we did in first grade?" Russell asks.

"Because when you're in the sixth grade, 'reading' as you call it, is taught as 'literature' in English class."

"Then why isn't it called literature class instead of English class?"

"That's just the way it is, Russell. Now, stand up and tell me what you remember about King Tut."

"He died," Russell says.

"Yes, we know he died, but what else can you tell us about him?"

"He was just a kid when they made him king, right?"

"Yes, he was very young, but you shouldn't refer to a king as a 'kid.' It isn't proper."

"I got a question. What's literature?"

"Blew, that's a very good question. Classic books that have been around for a long time are considered literature. Most have been written by people who died a long time ago but not always. Sometimes poetry is considered literature."

"I write poems," I lie. "But I sure didn't know I was writin' literature."

"You write poetry, Blew?" Miss Penny asks. I think I shocked her.

"Well, I only wrote one poem, and it ain't very long so I suppose it ain't literature." I'm tryin' to confuse Miss Penny 'cause I don't know one thing about that kid Tut, and I don't want her callin' on me and askin' about him.

"Is it a poem about King Tut?"

"Yes," I say. My lie's gettin' bigger.

"Excellent. Come to the front of the room and recite it for us. Pay attention, class. We may have another Longfellow among us."

"What's a Longfellow?" I ask.

"It's not a 'what' but a 'who.' Longfellow was a poet who lived many years ago. Perhaps next month we'll read some of his famous poems especially one called, 'The Song of Hiawatha.'"

"Did he write about the Hiawatha National Forest close to my house?" Larry asks.

"You'll have to read about his life and discover who and what he was writing about. Now, no more questions about Longfellow. Blew, come stand by my desk and recite your poem about King Tut."

"What if I don't remember all of it?" I'm stallin' for time.

"Recite what you do remember."

I clear my throat. I hope I can make up somethin' 'cause I wouldn't be caught dead writin' no poem. That's for girls and sissies. I wish I'd kept my mouth shut. I look around the room. Maybe I'll see somethin' that'll inspire me. I see Candy's hair, and I get an idea. "Here goes," I say. I cough again. "I call my poem 'Tut's Gum' and this is how it goes. 'Tut chewed some gum and it was fun until it got stuck in his hair. Then he pulled and tugged and hid under a rug 'cause his hair was now stuck in the air.' The end." The room is quiet until Russell laughs. Then Candy laughs and Johnny and then everybody.

"Class, stop laughing," Miss Penny commands. "That was a very nice poem. Thank you, Blew. Poems do not have to be long.

However, we're talking about King Tut. Johnny, what can you tell us?"

"Not much," Johnny mumbles. "I think he was a mummy."

"Well, at least that's something. Did your read the handout?"

"No."

"Then you might as well sit down. Flint, what can you tell me about King Tut?"

"He charmed snakes."

"Why do you say that?"

"Because he had magical powers."

"Was that in the handout?"

"No, Miss Penny. It was in the comic book I read last night."

"Sit down, Flint. You have no idea who King Tut was. Katie, I know you read the story. Stand up and tell the class all about King Tut."

"On this day in history a long time ago some people found the tomb where the King was buried," Katie says. "They were afraid to open the door because they thought something bad might happen to them because it isn't good to open anybody's grave. We all know that. You can't go poking around a cemetery whether it's in Egypt or Brimley or Sault Ste. Marie or Rudyard or anywhere. And King Tut had a really long name that nobody could pronounce so they shortened it to Tut. Maybe that was a nickname like we call Squeaky instead of Stephono. And King Tut loved birds, especially the kind that bury their head in the sand. And somebody said he had no heart, but I don't believe that because everyone has a heart. I think he died when he was a teenager. Maybe somebody killed him because they were jealous, but I'm not sure. He was rich."

"Well, Katie," Miss Penny says. "That was interesting but not quite correct."

"Would it be okay if I recited a poem I wrote?" Elizabeth asks.

"Is it about King Tut?"

"It could be."

"Then go ahead, Elizabeth. Recite your poem."

"Thank you. My poem is called 'The Needle' and it goes like this. 'Get your finger out of my eye, the needle cried and begged. I can't see to stitch or scratch an itch and it poked me real hard in the leg.' The end."

"I wrote one, too," Shirley says. "May I recite mine?"

"So did I. May I recite mine?" Candy asks.

"Well, it looks like King Tut Day is turning into poetry day. Blew, you started something."

"I guess so," I say.

"Shirley, please come to the front of the room and recite your poem."

"My poem is called 'Floating' and I think everyone will like it. Here goes. 'I'm watching a piece of lint float freely in the air. It's either lint or dandruff 'cause I just scratched it out of my hair.' The end."

"Very nice, Shirley. Now it's your turn, Candy."

"My poem isn't about King Tut or any person. It's one I wrote in homeroom this morning. When I looked out the window, the wind was blowing the leaves off the trees and that gave me an idea. My poem is called 'The Small Oak' and here goes. 'My small oak tree was sad today. All its leaves fell off. And as it rained and as wind blew I thought I heard it cough. Outside I ran into the cold and wrapped it in a rag, but all it did was shake its head and let its branches sag. I put my arms around its trunk and hugged it for awhile. Don't be afraid I told the bark and thought I saw it smile. An old pine tree stood next to it and whispered in the wind. It's autumn now and leaves must fall and oaks must sleep 'till spring.' The end."

"Excellent, Candy. That was an excellent poem. Perhaps one day you'll be a famous poet. Class, what did you think of Candy's poem?" Everyone claps except Flint.

"It was okay," he mumbles. "But mine's better."

"Flint, perhaps you have a case of the green-eyed monster. Recite your poem but be quick. The bell's about to ring."

Flint coughs as he walks to the front of the room. "My poem is called 'Mr. Worm.' Here goes. 'Mr. Worm your head's on a fern and your tail's stuck on my foot. Your body's gone, you're short not long, and you've lost your accordion look.' The end." Flint bows.

"Well, that certainly was different," Miss Penny says. "I think we're heard some very nice poems today, but we mustn't forget about King Tut. Tomorrow I'll get out the movie projector, and we'll watch a documentary about him. Then each of you will write a report."

The bell rings and everyone races out the door. Russell pounds me on the back. "Your poem was the best, Blew. Maybe you'll be a famous poet instead of Candy. And you fooled Miss Penny and got her off track. Nobody cares about that Tut kid."

"Thanks, Russell."

"Blew, your poem was stupid," Elizabeth says.

"Maybe it was stupid, but Russell's right. I fooled Miss Penny, and we didn't have to talk about Tut."

"You can't fool a teacher."

"Sure you can," Blew boasts. Just then Miss Penny walks by.

"What's that you were saying, Blew?" she inquires.

"Nothin'."

"That's what I thought," Miss Penny agrees. "You can't fool a teacher."

Chapter 13 – A Hunting Accident

Fenders doesn't hunt deer anymore. Two years ago he pulled the trigger on his rifle and shot something he shouldn't have. He hasn't hunted since. He promised to give me his rifle, but he didn't. He says he put it in its case and hid it where no one will ever find it. He says he'll never touch it again and just thinking about what he did makes him sick. He says he has nightmares and if he could go back to that day two years ago, he'd have stayed home. Instead of hunting today, he's sitting at our kitchen table.

"Squeaky, it was the saddest day of my life," he says to me. "If I live to be 100, I'll never forget seeing all that red snow."

"It wasn't your fault," I say. "It was an awful accident. The important thing is you didn't mean to do it."

"Nobody blames you," Daisy adds. "Not even Sims."

"I blame myself," Fenders says. "I was supposed to be running through the woods and driving the deer out instead of practicing my aim at a squirrel. It's my fault."

"Tell me the story," Elizabeth coaxes. "I've never heard it and neither has my brother."

"Ronnie, do you want to hear a story?" Fenders asks.

"Yes," Ronnie says. "I like stories."

"How old are you?"

"Almost six."

"I guess you're old enough."

"Tell your story in another room," Mom says. "We adults want to visit. Squeaky, take the kids to the back room."

I lead the way to the piano room. It's the best place to tell stories because Mom thinks it's haunted. She thinks the ghosts of dead people never left the room, but I don't believe in ghosts. I think Shirley does, but she'd never admit it. "Let's make a circle on the floor," I say. "It's cold in here and the closer we are, the warmer we'll be."

"You're not fooling us, Squeaky. You just want to sit next to Candy," Shirley teases.

"Never mind," Fenders says. "A circle is a good idea. Ronnie, since you're the youngest sit next to me and I'll tell the story. Our hunting tradition began long before I was born and will continue long after I'm dead. Traditions are like that. No one knows for sure when they started or when they'll end. Is everybody comfortable?" We nod and Fenders continues.

"Every November on the first day of hunting season we met early in the morning at Sims' place. He lives way back in the bush by the river. We don't see much of him unless he needs a ride to town or walks over to borrow a tool. He's a bachelor, and his only companion was his cat, Old Tom."

"What's a bachelor?" Ronnie asks.

"It's a man who never married," Fenders explains. "But no interrupting while I'm talking. You can ask questions when I'm done with my story."

"But I might forget what I wanted to ask," Ronnie whines.

"Then it wasn't very important. Now, keep quiet and I'll continue. That cat meant more to Sims than anything. Old Tom was a stray that wandered into his yard. He was half-dead from starvation, and Sims nursed him back to health. The bond between them was strong. I stopped by one time when Sims was frying pork chops. He invited me to sit down and eat. I had my eye on a juicy chop but before I could stab it with my fork, Sims speared it and tossed it to Old Tom."

"Why did Sims call him 'Old Tom'?" Ronnie inquires.

"Ronnie, stop asking questions," Elizabeth demands. "If you keep interrupting, we'll never hear the story."

"Did the cat eat the pork chop?" Ronnie asks. Fenders ignores him.

"Two years ago I was the first to arrive. The kitchen was hot so I loosened my jacket, straddled a chair, and waited for the others. One by one everyone walked in, all complaining about the cold. When the heat from the woodstove hit them, they took off their gloves and caps and hung their jackets on the back of their chairs. We drank coffee and discussed who would stand watch where, although we already knew because we followed the same tradition every year. Blew, Johnny, and Squeaky were told to leave their BB guns in the kitchen because I was the only hound allowed to carry a firearm."

"But you're not a hound. You're a man," Ronnie interrupts again.

"Please be quiet," Daisy says. "A hound is a feller who drives the deer out of the woods."

"That's crazy. Everybody knows you can't drive through the woods. Your car would get stuck."

"That's enough. Keep quiet." Elizabeth puts her hand over Ronnie's mouth. "Do you promise to keep quiet?" she asks. Ronnie nods his head, and Elizabeth removes her hand.

"When we were ready, we headed outside. Old Tom jumped from the top of the stack of wood next to the stove, and Sims let him out. As we walked through the field, he yelled at Old Tom to stay clear of the woods. 'Git back in the shed,' Sims hollered. As if he understood, the cat turned around. We watched as he made a beeline for the woodshed. The men who would do the shooting headed for their posts. The rest of us headed for the bush. We hooted and hollered to scare the deer out of their hiding places. If we didn't drive out a deer, we always told the same story. Sometimes we said they were just ahead of us or over the next hill or across the river. We always had an excuse for not driving one out."

"You mean you lied?" asks Ronnie. Fenders doesn't respond.

"Dad stood watch at the far corner of Fred's Bush. Mr. Clark and Mr. Quails watched at Tip's Knoll. Sims stood alone at the end of his property line. Blew and Squeaky drove west. Johnny and I drove south. Our section of the woods was mostly saplings so it was easy to see a deer, but none were in sight. Although the sun was out, there wasn't any heat in it. I was cold and wanted to go back, but Johnny said we had to keep going. We did for awhile, but then we stopped which wasn't a good idea because the cold settled around me like a blanket. When we saw Sims, we walked over to him. He asked if we were giving up. We said we were just taking a break. Then he started talking about his life. I knew the story by heart, but Johnny hadn't heard it.

"Sims said he was only a kid when his parents died from consumption, and he had to raise his brothers. He told us about fighting in World War II and the 81st Infantry called the Wildcats. The more he talked, the colder I got. I kept moving around to keep my blood circulating. Everything was quiet. We didn't hear Blew or Squeaky yelling. We figured they must have crossed the field and come out the far side closer to the bush where the men were waiting.

"Sims said the quiet reminded him of one morning when he saw four buddies shot down. He said they were the best Wildcats ever to draw breath. Then he asked what we thought about war. We said we didn't know because we'd never been in one. Then we said we'd better get back to the woods and drive out the deer. I wish I'd stayed with him." Fenders stops talking.

"Are you going to finish the story?" I ask.

"Squeaky, you know it as well as I do. I'm going home. You finish it." He gets up and walks towards the kitchen.

"You can't go now," Ronnie begs, but Fenders keeps walking. I know why he wants to leave. He doesn't like this room. It scares him and when he talks about Old Tom, he gets the willies. He told me when he was in here one time he heard a cat meow. When he called 'kitty, kitty' no cat came running, but the meowing continued. He thought it was the ghost of Old Tom following him. He said he often hears a cat cry when there's no cat around.

"Go ahead, Squeaky, and finish telling Elizabeth and Ronnie what happened. If you forget something, I'll remind you," Daisy says.

"Okay. Settle down, Ronnie. You can sit next to me if you want to."

"Sure do." He scoots next to me, and I continue the story. "When Fenders and Johnny left Sims, they didn't head back to the woods like they were supposed to. Instead, they headed towards his shack because Fenders was freezing cold. You know how skinny he is. Anyway, as they were walking Fenders saw a squirrel sitting on a fencepost. He took aim and fired his rifle. As soon as Sims heard the shot he ran towards us, but it wasn't a squirrel or deer he saw. It was Old Tom. Fenders was standing over him and watching the snow turn red as Old Tom lay dying. His blood froze as soon as it left his body."

"Fenders shot Mr. Sims' cat?" Ronnie can't believe his ears.

"Obviously," Elizabeth says. "Now be quiet. What happened next?"

"Sims asked why Fenders shot Old Tom, but Fenders didn't say anything. It was like he was in a trance so Johnny said it was an accident. He said Fenders was aiming at a squirrel, and Old Tom jumped in the way. The bullet got him instead of the squirrel that ran down the post and disappeared."

"Was Sims mad at Fenders?" Ronnie asks.

"It was hard to tell. Sims was mad and sad. Johnny kept saying it was an accident. That if Old Tom hadn't gotten in the way when Fenders pulled the trigger, it would be the squirrel that was dead, not the cat. Johnny tried to explain it was too late to stop the bullet once it left the barrel. Sims didn't say anything. Johnny said he was shaking his head as he watched Old Tom's black fur turn red. He said he picked him up and got blood all over his jacket. Fenders still didn't say anything, but Johnny said tears were rolling down his face. Johnny volunteered to help bury Old Tom, but Sims said the ground was frozen and the grave could wait. He started cooing to the cat just like a mother coos to her baby. Finally Fenders said he was sorry. Sims looked him in the eye and said he'd miss Old Tom, but he knew it was an accident. He said he was sure Fenders hadn't shot him on purpose. Then he told Fenders and Johnny to go home."

"Was it an accident?"

"Of course it was, Ronnie," I say.

"Maybe Fenders was mad because Old Tom got the pork chop he wanted."

"No, Ronnie. Fenders would never shoot anything other than a squirrel."

"How do you know for sure?"

"Because Fenders is kind."

"He wasn't kind that day," Ronnie whimpers.

"It was an accident," Katie explains.

"Yes, an accident," Shirley agrees.

"When I break my crayons on purpose, I tell my mother it was an accident," Ronnie confesses.

"Fenders didn't shoot Old Tom on purpose. Get that through your head," Elizabeth demands.

"Okay. If you guys say it was an accident then it was, but it sure sounds fishy to me."

Elizabeth pulls his ear until he howls. "That was no accident," she says. "Now do you know the difference?"

"I guess so," Ronnie admits. "But when I'm older, I'm going hunting. I hope a cat doesn't get in my way." Just then we hear a loud meow. I know our cats are in the barn, not in the house.

"Squeaky, I just heard a cat." Ronnie sounds scared.

"No," I say. "It was the wind." Nobody believes me and neither do I. We race for the kitchen. Fenders didn't go home. He's sitting at the table eating ginger snaps and drinking coffee.

"Did you finish the story, Squeaky?" he asks.

"Sure did," I say. "And I'm never telling it again."

Chapter 14 – The Parson's Nose and Buster

We've just eaten Thanksgiving dinner at my house. Flint and Squeaky are fighting in our living room, and I ask them to stop.

"Katie, we're not fighting," Flint says. "We're arguing."

"Sounds like fighting to me."

"It's all Flint's fault," Squeaky accuses.

"I didn't know you wanted that piece." Flint defends himself. "You should of let me know before I took it off the platter. I ain't no mind reader so there ain't no use gettin' mad at me."

"I ain't mad at you, but we ain't friends. We're through."

"C'mon, Squeaky. We're pals. We'll be pals no matter what. I'll even give you my cat eye marbles if you give me one steelie."

"No dice, Flint. We're done. There ain't no use talking 'cause nothing's gonna change my mind. We're done and that's that." The boys are in my living room. Squeaky's mad because Flint ate the parson's nose, Squeaky's favorite part of the turkey. I'm playing Old Maid with the girls. Fenders walks into the room.

"What's all the commotion?" he asks. "The adults are having coffee in the kitchen and enjoying themselves so you boys better stop fighting. They sent me in here to tell you to cut it out, you hear?"

"It ain't none of your business," Squeaky says. "We ain't fighting. We're just talking loud. Scram."

"Yeah, scram, Fenders. Mind your own business," Flint agrees with Squeaky.

"Well, you better not fight because it's Thanksgiving, and Katie's mother fixed a nice meal for everybody. I'm helping wash the dishes. If you don't behave, I'll tie an apron around your waists and you can wash the pots and pans." Fenders goes back to the kitchen.

"I'll give you one steelie if I can have all your cat eyes and two boulders," Squeaky suggests.

"Deal. We're friends again, right?"

"Sure, Flint, we're friends if you keep your end of the deal. Hey, Johnny. Wanna go outside with us and throw snowballs at the ram?"

"If you guys are going out, so are we," I say. We put away the cards and put on our warm clothes. The boys do the same and grab their BB guns. We go out the side door so we don't have to see our parents. We head for the barn.

"There's lots of snow," Blew says. "But it ain't packy so how we gonna make snowballs to throw at the ram?"

"Dig deeper," Johnny says. "There's packy snow underneath the new stuff."

"Good idea," Flint agrees. "Help me dig near this big pile."

"That big pile isn't snow," I say. "That's the manure pile."

"Well, Katie, it must have been that parson's nose that got me all mixed up. I sure don't want to dig in the manure pile."

"You know what a parson's nose on a turkey is, don't you?" asks Blew.

"Sure I do. It's the tastiest part of the bird. Everybody knows that."

"It's the rear end of the turkey." Everybody laughs.

"You're lying," Flint yells. He doesn't believe Blew.

"No, I ain't. I thought you knew what it was."

"I think I'm gonna be sick." Flint acts like he's going to throw up.

"You're okay." Squeaky comes to his rescue. "Blew's lying. Nobody would cook a turkey's butt when there's good stuff to eat like the legs and thighs and wings and all the white meat. Hey, look out. The ram's heading this way." We scatter as Buster lowers his head and chases us. The girls follow me up the ladder to the haymow. The boys run for the gate, but Buster chases Blew and pins him against the barn door. He can't move.

"Get him away from me," he yells. "He's crushin' my guts."

"Get him by the horns and give him a shove," Johnny yells. "Girls, throw down some hay. That'll get him off Blew." We push down a bale, and it lands on Buster's back. He shakes his head. Blew runs towards the gate, and the boys open it for him.

"Whew, that was close," Blew says. "I thought for sure I was a goner. Thanks, fellows. Thanks, gals for throwin' down the hay. You did good."

"You're safe, but we're not," I yell. "We're stuck up here until Buster goes away. Throw something at him so we can come down."

"Katie, there ain't nothing to throw," Flint hollers.

"Shoot him with your BB guns," Shirley suggests.

"He wouldn't even feel the BBs with all that wool on him," Johnny says. "C'mon fellows. Let's shoot some squirrels."

"You can't leave us in the haymow," Candy complains.

"You're all chickens," I say as the boys run to the pine trees behind the barn and fire shots at the squirrels.

"Katie, maybe the noise will scare Buster," Candy says in a hopeful voice, but when we look down Buster's eating the hay we threw at him.

"Looks like we're stuck up here until Papa comes to do the milking," I say. "We might as well tell stories. Who has a good one?"

"I do," Shirley volunteers. "But you have to promise not to get scared or tell anyone what I tell you. Promise?" Everybody agrees. Snooks, the cat, comes from her hiding place and sits on Shirley's lap as she tells her story.

"A long time ago Mom was picking blueberries at Dollar Settlement. She was just a little girl and wandered away from her mother. She saw an old man smoking a pipe. There was a big bowl of blueberries on his lap, but he wasn't eating them. He was stringing them on some wire wrapped around his neck. Mom got close to him and saw that they weren't blueberries at all, but little blue beads. The man smiled at her, then he disappeared."

"Where'd he go?" asks Candy.

"Mom said he vanished into the air like a puff of smoke. She watched him turn into a blue cloud and hang over the blueberry patch where her mother was. Then he reached down and grabbed her. Mom screamed but instead of sounds coming out of her throat, there was only blue blood dripping from her neck. She died and her spirit left her body near the sandy shore of Lake Gitche Gumee. That's what the Indians call Lake Superior. It was their lake a long time before it was ours. Their god gave it to them so they could fish and have lots to eat."

"That's awful," Candy says. "We stole their lake so they stole your mother. But she didn't really die because she's in Katie's house right now drinking coffee and eating pumpkin pie."

"Let her finish her story," I say.

"When the blue blood stopped coming out of her neck, she wasn't a little girl anymore. She was an old lady with long blue fingernails. At night she comes into my bedroom. She sits on the edge of my bed and smokes a pipe while she threads blue beads on a string."

"That's an awful dream," Candy says.

"I used to think it was a dream, but I'm not so sure anymore. Sometimes in the morning my bedroom smells like pipe smoke, and Pap doesn't smoke a pipe. I think an old spirit was in Mom when she was just a little girl, and it left her when she saw the old man. Spirits are real you know. Ask Larry when we're back at school. He knows about stuff like that because he's Indian."

"That doesn't make sense," I disagree. "Little girls don't have old spirits."

"Katie, we only see the outside of people. We can't see the inside."

"You mean spirits saw your mother's guts?" Candy asks.

"No, of course not. I'm talking about her inner spirit. The one that's hidden from everyone. The one that scares me whenever I pick blueberries at Dollar Settlement because I see an old man smoking a pipe. When I tell Mom, she says we're on hallowed ground and anything is possible."

"That's where the best berries are," I say. "They love the sandy ground."

"I know, Katie, and spirits never forget the past or that the white man picked all their berries and stole their lake and caught their fish. I think the old lady who comes to me is trying to warn me about something, but I don't know what."

"I think it's just a dream," Candy comments. "Sometimes I have crazy dreams, too."

"Does your bedroom smell like smoke when you wake up in the morning?"

"No."

"Then how do you know my dream isn't real?" Shirley asks a good question. Nobody talks as we think about this. Snooks stops purring, jumps from Shirley's lap, and runs back to her hiding place. Then we hear Blew calling.

"It's all clear, gals," he yells. "You can come down now. Buster's gone." Snow starts falling as we climb down the ladder, but instead of white flakes, they're blue. At least that's the color they look like to me.

"See what I mean," Shirley says. "The spirit that left Mom is showing us it's real."

"Hurry up," Flint hollers. "It's getting dark, and I don't feel so good. Must be that parson's nose trying to get out of my belly." I don't say anything, but I bet it isn't the parson's nose bothering Flint. I think it's his inner spirit trying to escape. I bet Shirley thinks so, too.

Everybody runs for my house. When we reach the porch, I stop and look at the sky. A blue cloud passes above us. I think I see an old lady with blue fingernails looking at me. It gives me the willies. Maybe Shirley told us the truth, but I don't want to believe it. If some of my dreams are real, I'm in big trouble.

Chapter 15 – Katie's Unlucky Day

Today was an unlucky day for two reasons. First, I couldn't get any music out of my clarinet. I blew and blew, but nothing came out except squeaks and moans and other strange noises. All the kids snickered, and I wanted to crawl into a hole and stay there. I hate band class, but I have to take it. I asked if I could play the drums, but Mr. Keller said no, drums were for boys. Our music teacher is young and bossy. He has one gold front tooth. He smells of Black Jack gum to hide the smell of cigar. He chews gum all the time, even during band practice. Nobody likes him because he's mean as a mangy dog.

I can't read clarinet notes, and I'm not going to learn. I wanted the drums, but he gave them to Larry. It's not fair. He didn't even want them. He wanted the trombone, but Mr. Keller gave that to Squeaky, who wanted the tuba which we don't have. I'll never last in this class. Mr. Keller might as well kick me out and get it over with. I'd rather spend an hour in the principal's office and wear the dunce cap than spend another ten minutes sucking a reed and blowing into the clarinet.

But bad as band was, it was nothing compared to what happened in arithmetic. Mrs. Messer is at least 90 years old and has no business trying to teach a room full of kids. Nobody likes her. She was on the warpath, marching back and forth in front of the blackboard and slapping the ruler in the palm of her hand. Something had riled her, and when she gets that way, she'd scare the hair off a donkey. She told us to keep our mouths shut and open our workbooks.

Johnny started teasing me like he always does. He sits across the aisle from me. He likes me more than I like him so he's always horsing around, trying to get my attention. We were writing in our workbooks, trying to figure out some long division problems.

Every time I wrote something, Johnny pushed my elbow making my pencil squiggle across the page. As soon as I erased the mess, he pushed my elbow again. I erased until there was a hole in my paper. Johnny saw it and started giggling on the inside. His shoulders shook, but his mouth kept quiet. The fifth time he pushed my elbow, I reached over and grabbed his pencil. Quick as a wink, I snapped it in two.

The room was quiet and the break sounded like a shotgun going off. Mrs. Messer clomped her big black ugly shoes over to my desk and lowered her head to mine. Her thick glasses magnified her eyes and drilled into mine. Her face looked like a dried up river bed with cracks and lines going every which way. She held it an inch from my face.

"Well, Missy. What's going on?" she demanded.

I was so scared I could feel the hair on my arms stand up. My heart was racing. I didn't dare look at Johnny for help. He's afraid of her, too. I never get into trouble, but I was all fired up about that awful clarinet business. I looked straight into Mrs. Messer's eyeglasses.

"Nothing," I said and my voice didn't even crack.

"Nothing? That shot we heard didn't sound like nothing. Sounded like you broke a pencil." She tapped out a Morse code warning with her clodhopper shoe.

"Yes, Ma'am, I did."

"Why?"

"I don't know."

"You don't know? You don't know or you won't tell me?" Her foot tapped louder and stronger on the wooden floor.

"I don't know, Ma'am."

"Then you know what's coming, don't you?"

"Yes, Ma'am." Mrs. Messer reached for the paddle hanging on a nail in the wall behind her desk.

"Bend over." I bent over and three whacks later I was a different person. "Give your pencil to Johnny," she said and then she marched me to a corner of the room and put the dunce cap on my head. "Let this be a lesson to you. The next time you break a pencil and I ask you a question, answer it. Do you hear me?"

"Yes, Ma'am."

"You can stand there until the bell rings."

I faced the corner and pretended I was invisible. Some kids get paddled almost every day, but this was the first time for me. I felt awful. I stood straight and tall and pretended my spirit left my body and was floating over the St. Marys River all the way to Sugar Island. I pretended I was an actress playing a part, waiting for a handsome prince to rescue me. That's how I endured the punishment. When school was over, Johnny walked me to the bus and said he was sorry he hadn't stuck up for me. I said it was okay. It didn't matter.

I sat in silence on the ride home and wouldn't talk to anyone, not even Blew or Flint when they tried to coax me into a good mood. When I got home, I told Mama what Mrs. Messer had done. She asked what I'd done to provoke her. I said as far as I knew, nothing. Mama gave me a hug. She said life was like that. Sometimes you got whacked for doing nothing at all, and I might as well get used to it.

I wonder if that's what happened to Mrs. Messer. I wonder if one of her teachers whacked her for doing nothing so she decided to become a teacher and do the same thing to her students. I bet that's the truth. Maybe I'll become a teacher and be mean to kids for no reason, but then again, maybe I won't. Maybe I'll become a principal and be mean to every teacher who picks on kids for no good reason. Mrs. Messer might still be a teacher when I'm the boss. I'll have a good laugh if she disobeys me. I'll make her wear the dunce cap and stand in a corner until her shaky old legs give out, and she falls in a heap to the floor. And when she sends a kid to my office, instead of punishing him, I'll feed him candy bars. I'll pat him on the shoulder and tell him not to worry, that I won't tell his parents and get him in trouble at home for something as simple as a broken pencil.

Well, it's nine o'clock. Time to turn off the light and go to sleep. Now that I have a plan, I feel better. I'm going to study real hard and become a principal and come back to torment Mrs. Messer if it's the last thing I ever do.

Chapter 16 – Scouting for a Christmas Tree

Elizabeth's dad volunteered to take us to Sugar Island so we could scout out Christmas trees. I told him we had plenty on my reservation, but he wouldn't listen. Even when Elizabeth said there were lots of trees on the sideroad, he still said the best ones were on the Island. I spent the night at Blew's house so Mr. Clout wouldn't have to drive to Bay Mills where I live. All the kids piled into the back of his pickup truck. Now we're in the Soo, waiting at the Sugar Island ferry dock.

"Larry, how do we get across the river?" Daisy asks me.

"The ferry will be here soon," I say. "Look over there. All the cars going to the Island just got off. Now the ferry will come back to this side and pick us up."

"Do we have to get out of the truck?" Squeaky asks.

"No, silly. Captain will drive us across," Elizabeth answers.

"Who's Captain?"

"He's my father, but I always call him Captain because that's what he is."

"My dad's a farmer, but I don't call him Farmer. I call him Papa," Katie says.

"My dad's a brick layer, but I don't call him Brick," Candy tells us.

"Captain's not my real dad so I usually just call him Captain."

"How many dads you got, Elizabeth?" Squeaky asks.

"My real dad and the dad Momma married, the Captain."

"You mean your real dad and real mother don't live together?"

"Ain't that what she just said?" Blew asks.

"They got a divorce when I was four. That's all I know, and I don't want to talk about it. The ferry's here."

We see a funny looking boat with a ramp so the cars and trucks can drive over the water and onto what looks like a fancy raft with a steel railing on both sides. Captain drives close to the front. If the ramp opens by mistake, we'll land in the river.

"Seems to me this is a lot of trouble to look for a tree when there's a million in my backyard," I say.

"Larry, it's an adventure," Elizabeth says. "Look at all the seagulls following us. They're waiting for the popcorn I brought. Take a handful and throw it on the water." Everyone sticks their hand in the bag and soon seagulls are everywhere. Their beaks are three inches long, and they screech at us as they grab the popcorn we throw at them.

"We have seagulls where I live, but they don't eat popcorn. They eat fish."

"These eat fish, too, Larry, but Captain thought it would be fun for us to feed them. Watch out, Blew. There's one aiming at your hat where some popcorn landed."

"Get away," Blew yells. He tries to punch the gull as it lands on his head, but he misses and it flies away with popcorn in its beak.

"Are you afraid of a seagull?" Flint asks.

"I ain't afraid of nothin', but I sure don't want no bird poop on my new hat."

"We're here," Elizabeth says. A worker lowers the ramp, and Captain drives over it. Now we're on a dirt road.

"Where's the sugar?" asks Daisy. "I don't see anything but trees."

"There isn't any sugar," Elizabeth explains. "Sugar Island is called that because lots of maple trees grow here. In the spring, people tap the trees and take the sap and boil it into syrup."

"You mean to tell me there ain't no sugar on this dang island? You mean to say we got up early and rode in the bed of Captain's truck and are freezin' and there ain't no sugar anywhere?" Blew sounds mad.

"I told you. We're having an adventure."

"Adventures are supposed to be fun. There ain't nothin' fun about this. I wanted to see the sugar trees. I thought that's why we came here. You tricked us."

"No, I didn't." Elizabeth defends herself.

"She didn't trick us." Daisy sticks up for her. "An adventure can be anything. I've never been on a ferry. Have you Blew?"

"Well, no, the ferry part was fun and all the noise from the horn, but I sure am disappointed there ain't no sugar cubes growin' on the trees or sugar canes growin' by the river."

"If you paid attention in class, you'd know sugar canes only grow in warm climates. You'd never see a sugar cane in the Upper Peninsula. Stop whining," Katie orders.

"Some of my people live on this Island," I say. "My dad said the Chippewa Indians were here first and called it Sisibakato Miniss. I ain't pronouncing the words right, but they mean Sugartree Island. White people can't speak our language so they saw all the maples and called it Sugar Island. They should have called it 'Sugar Tree Island.'"

"Thanks for the lecture, professor," Flint says. "I thought you were Ojibwe."

"People call us both, but don't ask me why because I don't know."

Captain turns down a long, bumpy lane. "Hang on, kids," he hollers out his window.

"Are we there yet?" Candy asks.

"Almost," Captain answers.

"I've been here lots of times," Elizabeth boasts. "Captain has a friend, Mr. Roi, who lives in a shack by the shore of the river. We can see Soo, Canada and maybe even an aquaplane land on the water."

"We can see Canada from my kitchen window," I say.

"You're right, Larry. And we can see Canada from the Michigan Soo," Flint adds. "We sure didn't have to come all this way to see an old man in a shack by the shore when we can see the same thing in Brimley."

"I told you we're having an adventure."

"Well, Elizabeth, it better hurry up because I'm cold," Daisy complains.

Finally Captain stops the truck and we hop out. Mr. Roi has gray hair and a gray beard. He's standing on his porch and telling us to come in. When we step inside his shack, we see four Christmas trees all with weird decorations on them.

"Welcome," Mr. Roi smiles at us. "Merry Christmas. Are you kids ready for some fun?"

"Yes," everyone yells.

"Then before you start looking for the trees you want, start looking for the popcorn balls I hid. You can look in every room except my bedroom."

"What about the toilet?" Flint asks.

"Toilet's outside," Mr. Roi says. "You can look there if you want to, but you won't find a popcorn ball in the outhouse."

We take off our jackets and boots and line them up by the woodstove. Captain and Mr. Roi sit at the table. We hunt everywhere. Even the dog joins us and starts barking. Mr. Roi yells, "Hammer, stop that racket. These kids are company." Hammer obeys. We follow him to a far corner of the room where he's sniffing around an old trunk.

"Get away from that trunk," Mr. Roi yells again, but Hammer keeps sniffing and starts barking. The popcorn balls must be in it. I'm about to lift the lid when Mr. Roi warns, "Don't touch that lid, kid, or you'll be sorry."

"Larry, maybe somebody's buried in the trunk. Open the lid," Flint dares me.

"Get away from it," Candy begs. "I don't want to see a dead body."

"Open it," Blew demands. "Don't be a fraidy cat."

"Just peek in it," Squeaky suggests. "I'll stand behind you so Mr. Roi can't see."

"We're guests here," Elizabeth reminds us. "Leave the trunk alone, Larry. Let's search around the trees."

I have to agree with her. "Elizabeth's right," I say. "If Mr. Roi doesn't want us snooping in his trunk, we better obey him." I move away from it, but it must contain something smelly because Hammer's still sniffing and scratching it. Dogs smell things humans can't. Mr. Roi might have put food in there. He might be trying to trick us into thinking there's something scary in it.

"You're a chicken, Larry." Flint points his finger at me.

"No more chicken than you are."

"Hey, look," Katie yells. "There's a pile of balls hidden behind that big tree with the beer can on top." Everyone runs to the tree. The popcorn balls are small and homemade and wrapped in colored paper. There's enough for every kid to have two.

"Okay, kids, you found your treat. Now it's time to find your Christmas trees."

"Why do you have so many in here?" Squeaky asks.

"There's one for each season," Mr. Roi says. "Notice how they're decorated. Winter has white ornaments. Spring has green. Summer has yellow. Fall has all the colors of autumn leaves."

"Good idea," Katie remarks. "I wish we could have four trees in our house, but there's not enough room."

"You could have little trees," Elizabeth suggests. We ignore her. Nobody wants four spruce trees in their house. Sometimes white people don't know much about anything.

"That sure is a pretty dog," Daisy says. "I've never seen a red one before." Hammer is begging for a popcorn ball. He stopped making a fuss about the trunk.

"He's an Irish Setter," Mr. Roi explains. "He's supposed to be a hunting dog, but he spends most of his day just sitting around. He's good company, though. You kids got names?"

"I'm Larry," I say and everyone gives their name.

"I'll remember Larry because he's the one who wanted to open the trunk, but I won't remember all the other names so I'll just call you kids. How's that?" We agree and sit on the floor while we eat our popcorn balls and admire Mr. Roi's trees. He did a good job decorating them. Then we're ready to go outside.

Mr. Roi tells us he made a trail with his snowshoes and if we follow it, we won't get lost. He hands me a ball of binder twine and a pair of scissors. When we find the trees we want, we'll wrap the twine around them. I'm the leader because everyone knows Indians are good scouts. We start down the snowshoe trail. There are lots of trees but most are maples with a few spruce sprinkled among them. As we walk, I'm on the lookout for animal tracks. I know bears and moose live on the Island. I see lots of squirrel and partridge tracks, but so far no bear tracks. I suppose they're hibernating for the winter.

"What about that tree," Blew yells.

"Too big," I say.

"It doesn't look too big," Blew argues.

"That's because it's surrounded by maples. They make it look small."

"Well, how about that one over there?" asks Katie.

"Too scrawny."

"This one looks perfect," Elizabeth points to one.

"It's about the right size, but it's a white pine. They don't make good Christmas trees."

"Why not?"

"They're too hard to decorate. See the long needles? You'd never get an ornament hung on them."

"We've walked a mile," Flint grumbles. "There ain't no good trees on this Island just like there ain't no sugar. Let's turn back."

"Not yet," Elizabeth says. "Captain won't like it if we don't find at least one tree."

"Flint's right. There ain't no good ones here," Blew grunts. "This is a wild goose chase."

"And Mr. Roi's trail is running out," Squeaky adds. "We're going to get lost if we don't turn back."

"Don't be a chicken," Katie says. "Larry's our scout. Indians know how to scout without getting lost. Right, Larry?"

"Sure thing," I say, but as soon as we lose the trail one tree looks the same as the next. It's easy to get turned around, but I won't tell my friends I don't know which direction to take. "Follow me. We'll find the right tree."

"One tree ain't no good," Blew says. "We need six. One for each of us."

"Six won't fit in the truck today," Elizabeth explains. "Captain will come back tomorrow and chop down the trees and deliver one to each of us."

"What if I don't want the tree he gives me, but the one I picked out?" Daisy asks. "What if you get Flint's tree and he gets yours and Candy gets mine and I get Larry's and he gets Squeaky's? What about that, Elizabeth?"

"I don't know."

"This was a dumb idea," Blew announces. "I'm goin' back."

"Me, too," Daisy says. "My foot hurts. This isn't fun, and it isn't an adventure. I want to go home."

"Hey, guys. Look over there by the dead cedar. That's the perfect tree."

"You're right, Larry," Flint says. "And it's mine." He runs towards it.

"I saw it first." I run after Flint, Daisy hobbles after me, Squeaky and Blew run past me, and Elizabeth screams it's only fair it's hers because Captain drove us to the Island.

"Stop," I command when we reach the tree. "Ain't nobody getting this one. Look at all the tracks around it. A partridge lives under its branches. That's why it's the perfect tree. Partridges always pick the best one to winter under away from predators."

"Then why'd you tell us we could have it?" Squeaky asks.

"I didn't see the tracks until now. We're leaving this spruce right where it is."

"Fiddlesticks," Daisy says. "This is stupid. A million trees on this Island and the only one we find is home to a partridge. We might as well tie some pears to the boughs and have a real partridge in a pear tree."

"You might be right," I laugh. "Let's go back. Tomorrow we'll find our own trees on our own land, and we won't have to fight about who gets the best one. Follow me." We turn around and I find the trail.

"You kids back already?" Mr. Roi asks. "Did you find the trees you wanted?"

"We sure did," Katie says. "And they're the ones in our own backyards."

"That's the way it usually goes," Mr. Roi agrees. "That's where most things are. Right before our eyes if only we could see them. Come in and warm yourselves before Captain takes you home."

We go in and stand around his woodstove. Mr. Roi must have found the only trees on Sugar Island that are perfect for Christmas. I think he and Captain were teaching us a lesson. Like my dad always says when I complain we're not rich like other folks. He says I'm supposed to find riches in my family that have nothing to do with money. I guess maybe he's right. Captain goes outside and starts the truck. He tells us our adventure is over and to hop aboard.

"You kids come back in the spring when the sap's running," Mr. Roi says. "I'll show you how to turn it into maple syrup."

We wave and promise we'll be back if Captain will bring us. Then we take our places and wrap blankets around us. Flint starts talking about Mr. Roi's trunk.

"Must have been something mighty special. Something Mr. Roi didn't want us to see," Katie says.

"I bet it was a skull," Squeaky suggests.

"Or maybe the corpse of his dead wife." Flint makes his voice sound scary.

"Mr. Roi doesn't have a wife," Elizabeth snaps.

"Not any more," Flint laughs. "I bet he chopped her by mistake when he was chopping down all those Christmas trees. He didn't have time to bury her so he hid her in the trunk."

"You're crazy, Flint," Daisy says. "And you're scaring me."

"It might have been an accident. I bet she was standing in his way when he swung the axe and chopped off her head."

"You could be right, Flint," Blew agrees. "Or it could be that's where he hides the dog treats."

"Yeah, that's probably what it was, but it sure would be more interesting if there was a person hidden in the trunk."

"For sure, Larry. Gives me the creeps just thinking about it." Everyone's quiet until Flint yells, "Boo. Scared you, didn't I?" I'm the first one to punch him. Then the other kids join in and we laugh as we head towards home.

Chapter 17 – The Christmas Play

"Daisy, this will be our last Christmas play," I say. "They don't have these things in seventh grade. I hope this year I get to be a person and not a donkey like last year. For sure I don't want to be in the choir. Mr. Keller knows I can't sing so maybe he'll choose me for one of the wise men."

"Blew, I don't care who I am, but I don't want to be Joseph," Russell says. "All he does is sit next to Mary and look at the kid in the manger."

"Russell, you can't call baby Jesus a kid," Daisy reprimands.

"Oh, don't be so fussy. It's only a doll. It ain't a real baby."

"That's not the point," Daisy disagrees. "If the play is to seem real, we must pretend the doll is real or nobody will believe us."

"Nobody believes us anyway," Katie says. "It's all pretend. Last year Shirley brought a girl doll. We pretended it was a boy."

"That was different. The manger was facing Mary and Joseph so nobody knew Jesus was a girl. And besides, the doll was bald and so are all babies."

"Not so, Daisy," Russell says. "My aunt's baby had more hair on his head than his pa. Ain't that a fact, Blew? You saw him didn't you?"

"Yes," I lie. I ain't never been to his house because he lives miles away from Brimley, but us fellers gotta stick together.

"Well, most babies are bald," Candy says. "I want to play Mary. I know she doesn't have any lines, but she's the prettiest one in the play."

"Katie was Mary last year. She wore an old blue sheet that looked like a rag, plus she forgot to take off her glasses. She sure looked stupid sittin' on that bale of hay and pushin' up her glasses. Mary didn't wear glasses because they hadn't been invented yet," I say.

"Well, Blew, I don't wear glasses, and I have a new blue sheet Mommy bought in case Mr. Keller picks me. Mommy said I can wrap her best white scarf around my head just like Mary would have worn." Candy gives me a lecture.

"You don't know what she wore on her head," Russell says. "She might have wore a turban."

"Yeah, like Aladdin," I say.

"Aladdin didn't wear a turban and for sure Mary didn't. She wore a nice scarf just like I will if I'm picked to play her."

"Aladdin did so wear a turban," Russell yells. "There's a picture of him in a book I have at home."

"Well, I know for sure Mary didn't," Candy says. "I don't care what Aladdin wore on his head. He isn't real."

"He could be. How do we know Mary and Joseph and their kid are real?" I ask. "They could be as phony as Santa Claus."

"What did I hear you say, Blew?" asks Mr. Keller as he walks into the room.

"Nothin'," I say.

"We were discussing the Holy Family," Candy explains. "And who you might pick to play Mary. I don't wear glasses, and I don't mind not having any lines. And this will be my last Christmas play unless I flunk sixth grade and that's not very likely. "

"I've been thinking about who will play the various roles," Mr. Keller says. "You might get your wish, Candy, but don't be disappointed if you don't. Remember, Mary had brown hair, not red like yours, and nobody has any lines except the angel announcing the birth."

"I could wear a brown wig," Candy suggests. "Or maybe Mommy's scarf would cover all my hair and nobody would know it's red."

Mr. Keller don't say nothin'. He walks to his desk and opens a drawer. Then he unwraps a piece of gum and starts chewin'. The bell rings and the rest of the kids hurry into the room. Finally Flint walks in. He's late for almost every class, and the teachers never yell at him. If I'm late once, they yell so loud somebody'd think I had set the hall on fire.

"Class, as you all know, today I decide who will play the major roles in our Christmas pageant. I've decided to use the democratic method so I'm putting everyone's name in this box. The first name I pull out will play Joseph." He sticks his hand in the box and takes out a slip of paper. "Well, Candy. It looks like you're Joseph."

"I can't play Joseph. I'm a girl. I want to play Mary." Candy's almost cryin'.

"Too bad," Mr. Keller says. "The next name will be for Mary. You missed your chance, Candy." Mr. Keller makes a big show of mixin' up the names. Then he pulls out another slip of paper. "Well, well. Howard Crisp will be playing Mary." Everyone laughs.

"I can't play Mary," Howard yells. "It's gotta be a girl."

"Switch with me Howard." Candy hands him her slip of paper.

"Good idea," Howard says. "We'll switch."

"Now, now, class, settle down and stop laughing. This is a democracy and what I say goes. Howard, we'll find you a wig and a blue sheet, and no one will notice you're a boy. Candy, Howard will be sitting on the hay and you'll be standing. Nobody will notice you're a girl."

"Mrs. Hubbard says a democracy is where everyone gets a vote. I say we vote to see who wants a boy to play a girl and a girl to play a boy," Howard suggests.

"Mrs. Hubbard is right," Mr. Keller responds. "But for every rule there's an exception. You will play Mary and Candy will play Joseph and that's final. The third name I pull out will play the angel." He puts his hand in the box again and pulls out Russell's name. "It's you, Russell."

"I can't play the angel because I stutter. People will laugh at a stuttering angel."

"Russell, you only have one line. We'll have plenty of time to rehearse until you can say it without stuttering. And just when did this stutter develop? I've never heard about it until now."

"I don't stutter when I play the trumpet. That's why you've never heard me. For sure, I'll stutter in front of a bunch of parents. Please, Mr. Keller. Please pick someone else."

"No, Russell. You're the angel. You'll do fine. As a matter of fact, you didn't stutter when you were talking right now so I think you've already overcome your problem. Let's continue and see who will play the wise men. I'll pick out three slips of paper.

Okay, looks like it will be Johnny, Larry, and Squeaky. We'll figure out who carries in which gift when practice begins. Now I'll pick out names for the animals. First is Katie. You'll be the donkey. Next is Elizabeth. You'll be a sheep. Third is Shirley. You'll be a cow. Fourth is Daisy. You'll be an ox. I think that's enough animals to fill the stage. The rest of the class will be in the choir to the left of the main participants. Any questions?"

Everybody starts complainin'. The room sounds like it's full of magpies. I don't say a word in case Mr. Keller changes his mind. Now I'm glad I'm in the choir. I won't have to sing. All I have to do is move my lips and pretend. Just like nobody will know Howard's a boy and Candy's a girl, nobody will know I'm not singin'. I think I'm gonna have a lot of fun at our last Christmas play. Things are sure lookin' up. I ain't called Blew for nothin'. I must of blew some new ideas into Mr. Keller's mind to make him turn our play upside down.

Chapter 18 – A Balsam Tree for Katie

Papa promised to get our Christmas tree this morning. I want a balsam because their needles don't pick as much as a spruce tree, and they smell better.

"I always liked balsams, Katie," Grandpa says. "If I was younger, I'd go with you. I'd drive the tractor as fast as the wind." Grandpa's in a good mood. I guess he found the last of Granny's dandelion wine.

I put on my jacket and step outside. Blew, Flint, and Johnny are helping Papa throw a ladder, shovels, and a saw in the cart. Papa starts the tractor and hitches the cart behind it. We hop in and Lard joins us. We start singing "Jingle Bells" as Flint snaps an invisible whip at the invisible reindeer.

The road's slippery and the tractor's chains dig into the ice. We pass the big spruce tree that has my name on it. Blew painted our names on two trees, but his tree got struck by lightning last fall and crashed to the ground. Just past my tree, Papa turns the tractor into a narrow path leading through the woods to the pasture where our beef cows summer. They're in the barn now because it's too cold for them to stay in the field. Papa drives slowly as we look at the trees.

"There! There!" I yell. "There's a good one." A giant balsam towers above us. Its branches are covered with snow. Papa stops the tractor.

"Katie, are you sure you want this one?" he asks. "It looks mighty big, and it's not a spruce."

"Yes, yes. That's the one! Please, Papa."

"Well, if you're sure. What do you boys think?"

"I think it's a mighty big tree, but if Katie wants it, I guess it's the right tree," Flint says.

"It sure is big," Blew agrees. "You could make a lot of skis from it."

"Or make it into logs and build a fence to keep the pigs in," Johnny suggests.

"I don't care what you do with it after it's done being our Christmas tree," I say.

Papa hands shovels to the boys. They make a circle around the balsam. Papa gets the ladder and leans it against the tree. He takes the saw and climbs up the ladder. "We'll top her off," he yells. "She's too tall to take all of her. Stay clear of the tree. I'm almost through the trunk." We watch as the top of the tree leans to one side and falls to the ground.

The smell of fresh cut balsam fills the air. Papa comes down the ladder and helps brush off some of the snow. I find a bird's nest among the branches. It survived the fall and feels like it's made of cement instead of twigs and mud. We help Papa drag the tree to the cart, hop on, and head for home. When we get there, Mama opens the door. We drag the tree through the kitchen and front room and lean it against the wall. Blew and Papa put it in a stand, but it still looks shaky. It might topple over at any minute. If it falls, it won't be the first Christmas tree to crash to the floor.

"Here's some heavy twine to anchor it." Mama hands Papa the ball of twine. He winds some around a nail in the wall. Then he runs the string through the boughs to the other side of the wall where there's another nail.

"Done," Papa says.

"Move it to the left," Grandpa suggests.

"Move it to the right," Blew orders.

"It's gonna fall," Flint yells.

"There's a big hole where there are no branches," I notice.

"It's going to stay where it is and that's final," Papa says. "Katie, pour some water in the stand and give this balsam a drink." He moves away from the wall and looks at the tree. "It looks good," he says and finally everyone agrees.

"Where's the decoratin' stuff?" Blew asks.

"Before we decorate, I want the boys to shake the snow off the branches," Mama says. "Katie, run to the pantry and find some rags to put underneath the tree to catch the snow as it melts. I'll make hot cocoa."

"I'll put away the tractor and be back in a few minutes. Boys, don't try to put the angel on the top of the tree. Remember what happened last year." We all groan. Last year Blew tried to lift Flint onto his shoulders, but they fell forward and crashed into the tree. They didn't knock it down, but they broke lots of ornaments and made a big mess. They promise not to do the same this year. When the cocoa is ready, Mama brings it in and passes around the cups. Papa comes in and takes a cup topped with lots of marshmallows. When "Rockin' Around the Christmas Tree" comes on the radio, we put down our cups and dance, even the boys and even Grandpa. Then we finish decorating the tree and the boys go home.

"Are you happy with the balsam?" Mama asks. I look at the tree and know I have to tell the truth.

"I guess so, but it sure is a puny old thing. It looked a whole lot better in the woods. Maybe that's where it should have stayed." Mama doesn't say anything, but a grin spreads across her lips.

"Katie, next year we'll get a spruce," she says. "That's always been our tradition."

I don't like to admit it, but Mama's right. I guess it's not a good idea to mess with tradition.

Chapter 19 – New Year's Resolutions

"Welcome back, children," Mrs. Lark says. "Did everyone have a wonderful Christmas vacation?"

"No," everybody yells. Before Mrs. Lark came into the room, Blew told us to say we had a lousy vacation if she asked.

"My goodness, children. That's not the answer I expected. Who wants to tell me why you didn't have fun during your two weeks off?"

"I'll tell you why," Blew says. "Because Santa didn't bring me the horse I ordered. Mr. Sims has a nice Arabian for sale, and I wanted it and I wrote to Santa and he ignored my list. I didn't get the horse or the saddle or real cowboy boots or anythin' that was on my list."

"Maybe next year," Mrs. Lark says. Larry raises his hand. "Yes, Larry. What was wrong with your vacation?"

"Santa didn't bring me a pair of hockey skates that I asked for, and I'm stuck with my old ones that are falling apart and dull as the books Miss Penny makes us read."

"Maybe Santa will bring you a new pair of skates next year. Who's next?"

"I asked for another doll, but all I got was a pair of socks," Shirley complains.

"I asked for a transistor radio, but all Santa brought me was one comic book," Russell grumbles.

"Santa left me a pair of pajamas instead of the pink angora sweater I wanted," Elizabeth whines.

"Santa didn't read my list. All he gave me was underwear," Flint moans.

"I've heard enough complaints so you might as well put down your hands," Mrs. Lark commands. "First of all, there's not one student in here who believes in Santa Claus. Secondly, I think you're all teasing me. I know everyone had a nice vacation because there was no school. Be satisfied with the gifts you were given. Now, what are your New Year's resolutions? Blew, since you were the first to complain, what resolution have you made for 1958?"

"I resolve never to lie again," Blew lies.

"That's an excellent start. Daisy, what's your resolution?"

"I resolve to dust the upstairs every Saturday."

"That's a good resolution. Flint?"

"I resolve to never cuss again as long as I live on this blasted earth."

"That resolution is worthwhile even if you did cuss as you were resolving it. Who's next? Russell?"

"I resolve to never again copy spelling words off anybody's paper, not that I do now but just in case I get the urge to in the future."

"Excellent resolution. If you write each spelling word five times, you'll never have to copy. You'll have the words committed to memory. Danny?"

"I resolve to make new friends and not forget my old ones in Paradise."

"Very good, Danny. Class, Danny Springs moved to Brimley from Paradise. I hope you make him welcome."

"I thought Paradise was in heaven," Blew says.

"It is," Mrs. Lark responds. "But there's also a small town in Michigan called Paradise. Danny, would you like to tell the class about your town?"

"No, but I will if you make me."

"I won't make you, but I thought the class might like to hear about Paradise."

"It's like every small Upper Peninsula town. There's not much to it except bars and churches." Everybody laughs.

"You got that right," Blew says. "Welcome to Brimley."

"Thank you," Danny replies. Then everyone starts talking and saying they want to hear all about Paradise.

"Does Paradise have a Garden of Eden?" asks Elizabeth.

"Does it have fig trees?" Candy wants to know.

"Does it have snakes?" Daisy shudders.

"Does it have apple trees?" Shirley inquires.

"Now, children. Stop asking Danny silly questions. It's almost time for your next class. I'm going to ask you one more time. Did everyone have a nice Christmas vacation?"

"No," we all yell. The bell rings and we're out the door before Mrs. Lark can holler at us. Danny bumps into me.

"Excuse me," he says.

"That's okay. I'm Katie. Do you like your new home?"

"I guess so."

"We have arithmetic now. Do you like it?"

"Yes. Do you?"

"No, I hate it because it doesn't make sense. I love English. Here's our room. Our teacher is Mrs. Messer. She's mean."

"Maybe she's not mean, just strict," Danny says. "The school in Paradise was only one room and all the kids from kindergarten to the eighth grade were in it so our teacher had to be strict to maintain order."

"Well, maybe you're right, but the other teachers are nice except Mr. Keller our music teacher. He made Candy be Joseph and Howard be Mary in our Christmas play. Candy was okay, but Howard was so embarrassed he said he wasn't going to show up, but his mother made him. He kept his head down and stared at the doll in the manger. The kids still tease him and call him 'Mary.' Don't tell him I told you. He might get mad at me. He's my boyfriend."

"You have a boyfriend?"

"Yes, but Howard doesn't know it and don't tell him."

"Quiet, people," Mrs. Messer says. "Did everyone have a nice Christmas vacation?"

"No," everybody yells. What a way to start the New Year— with a big fat lie. We loved our presents and best of all, we loved having no school for two whole weeks.

Chapter 20 – The January Thaw

"Anybody home?" Blew pounds on our kitchen door as he throws it open. "Hello everybody," he yells and turns to me. "Katie, get your skates on. If you don't hurry up, this old January thaw will turn our rink to mush. Flint and Johnny are already skatin' so let's go. Goodbye, everybody." Blew never speaks in a normal voice. He yells at the top of his lungs.

I pull on my snow pants and boots, zip my jacket, gather my mittens, hat, and scarf, and take my skates from the hook behind the woodstove. They're warm, but they won't stay that way for long. "Be careful," Mama says, but I'm already out the door and heading for the rink. The boys did a good job of cleaning it. I sit on the wooden bench Papa made for us, take off my boots, and lace up my skates.

I glide over the ice and pretend I'm a famous skater. Blew and the boys want to play hockey, but I want to practice stopping. The only way I can stop is to skate into the snowbank around the rink. "Help me," I ask Flint, but he shakes his head. I won't ask Johnny because he likes me, but I don't like him. I guess I'll keep skating in circles until I get tired or crash into the bank. There's a rink at school and some days I take my skates with me. Howard tries to help me stop, but we usually end up falling because I trip him. Everybody on the rink laughs and so do we. Lots of kids can't stop unless they fall.

"Katie, you gonna hog the rink all day?" Blew asks. He's holding his hockey stick and pretending he's Gordie Howe as he passes the puck to Flint and Johnny. "C'mon boys, let's play." They're on my rink every day even when the temperature drops below zero. They play hockey and it makes me mad. I thought this rink was supposed to be mine. I complained to Papa, but he laughed and said the boys were having fun. He said they could teach me how to play hockey, but I don't care about that. Everybody knows hockey is for boys. It isn't long before Candy joins us.

"Katie, have you learned to stop without plowing into the snowbank?" she asks. "Want me to show you how it's done?"

"Yes," I say. She holds out her hand and yells at the boys. "Get out of our way or we'll run over you." The boys obey and skate to the other side of the rink.

"We'll skate in a circle a few times," she says. "When it's time to stop, just stick the sharp point of your skate into the ice like this." She shows me how to do it. Then we go around the rink faster and faster until she shakes off my hand, races ahead, and stops like a real skater. The boys clap and whistle. When she shakes off my hand I'm not ready so, of course, I fall. The boys laugh and skate over to me. Six hands reach out to help me, and I grab the nearest ones. Guess who I got—Johnny. Then the boys chase Candy and me around the rink. Around and around we go and with every circle we make, our blades dig deeper and deeper into the ice. Finally Blew yells.

"This is crazy. We're ruinin' the rink. Everybody off." I don't know why, but we obey him. We skate to the bench, unlace our skates, and look at the rink. It's a mess.

"There's nothin' worse than a January thaw," Blew complains.

"You're right about that," Flint agrees.

"You boys know what you're talking about," Johnny says.

"If it wasn't for the January thaw how could we ever survive winter?" Candy asks. "It's been snowing since October, and it won't stop until after Easter. Enjoy the warmth." She leans back and looks at the sun. "I'm going to get a tan," she says and we laugh. Whoever heard of getting a tan in January in Michigan's Upper Peninsula? We put on our boots, sit awhile, and the boys talk about cleaning the rink before it freezes and all our ruts ruin the ice. Mama brings us hot cocoa.

"You're the best," Blew tells her.

"You're better than the best," Flint flatters her.

"You're tops," Johnny agrees.

Mama smiles at the boys. Sometimes I think she's glad to have them around because they always thank her and tell her she's pretty. Boys are like that. They're sneaky, at least that's what

Elizabeth says. She says boys will tell you anything just so they can copy off your homework or peek at your spelling words during a test. Maybe she's right because she sure is popular with all the boys.

We finish drinking our cocoa. Mama, Candy, and I head for the house, but the boys grab shovels and start scraping the rink. Maybe it is a good idea to have them around. It's nice to share what you have with other people especially when they do the work for you. I look back and see the boys struggling with the heavy shovels and slush. A smile spreads across my lips. I can't wait until the January thaw passes and the rink freezes nice and smooth again.

"Keep at it boys," I yell. "You're doing a great job." Candy and I run ahead of Mama. I turn around and yell again. "Give it all you've got, boys. Give it all you've got. This thaw won't last forever." The boys wave. Mama smiles. She knows what I'm doing. Praise the boys, and they'll do all the work for you. Candy and I laugh all the way to the house. Boys sure are stupid.

Chapter 21 – The Snowball Fight

"What special day was February 1?" asks Miss Penny.

"Robinson Crusoe Day," everyone yells.

"Very good, class," she says. "Johnny, tell us what you know about Robinson Crusoe." Johnny doesn't know much about anything except pigs because his pa's a pig farmer. He stands up quick as a wink. There's a big smile on his face.

"Robinson Crusoe loved pigs. When his boat crashed, all the pigs on board swam to shore. Robinson had bacon for breakfast, ham sandwiches for lunch, and pork belly for supper. What else do you want to know?" Everybody laughs even Miss Penny. She's not as mean as she used to be. Maybe she got a good Christmas present.

"Johnny, how do you know pigs were on the Esmeralda?"

"What's the Esmeralda?" Johnny asks. "Was it the raft Robinson clung to when he swam to shore?"

"Sit down, Johnny," Miss Penny says. "You have no idea who Robinson Crusoe was. Sit down and listen to your classmates who have read Mr. Defoe's story. Daisy, what can you tell us about Mr. Crusoe?"

"Robinson Crusoe was a famous man who sailed the ocean blue in 1842. He found America, home of the free and land of the brave. He also was the first pitcher for the Detroit Tigers, at least I think that's who he was." Miss Penny tells Daisy to sit down and get her facts straight. Her face turns red as a radish.

"Katie, we all know you read the story. Stand up and tell the class who Mr. Crusoe was." This is my chance to show off. All the kids are watching, expecting me to spout off about Crusoe, the castaway, and his adventures in Trinidad and cannibals and pirates. It only takes a minute for me to decide what I'm going to do. I stand as tall as a soldier waiting to be shot. I stand and stare right into Miss Penny's trusting eyes. I don't blink as I tell a lie so big it makes Blew's lies look puny.

"Robinson Crusoe was the son of John the Baptist," I announce. "He found China when Queen Elizabeth asked him to take the train to Buffalo. He cooked pigs' feet over a campfire made from the bones of gorillas." By now the kids are laughing so loud I can hardly keep a straight face, but I keep going. "Crusoe shot President Lincoln because Lincoln's big head was in the way, and he wouldn't take off his hat and Crusoe wanted to see the play. When he was little, he...."

"Sit down, Katie," Miss Penny says. She shakes her head. "I don't know what's gotten into everyone today, but it must be the weather. Too much winter snow and ice have frozen your brains. Open your readers to Robinson Crusoe." Everyone opens their book. Some kids read with their fingers so they won't lose their place. I feel sorry for them. It must be awful. Imagine if they had no fingers. How would they ever learn to read? Miss Penny stands at the front of the room and reads to us. She uses different voices for all the different parts. She's at the good part when the bell rings. It's time for recess. Once we're outside, a bunch of kids gather around me. "You were great, Katie," Shirley says. "You were smart to act as silly as the other kids."

"Way to go, Katie." Danny pats me on my back. "I'm sure you know who Crusoe was, but it was clever of you to make up such a funny story."

Blew throws a snowball at me. "Hey Katie, you sure surprised Miss Penny with the stupid stuff you were sayin'. It ain't true, is it?" Danny throws a snowball at Blew and hits him on the arm.

"You're the best," hollers Johnny. "You're the smartest girl in class." He grins at me. I throw a snowball at him and hide behind the fort. He throws a ball at me but misses.

"Katie, why'd you make up that story?" Elizabeth asks. She throws a snowball at Johnny.

"I don't know. I forgot it, but I had to say something." The kids know I'm lying, at least I hope they know. Nobody would be dumb enough to think I thought Robinson Crusoe, a made-up character from a book, shot Lincoln.

"Look out," yells Shirley, but it's too late. A giant snowball flies towards our fort and hits Squeaky right between his eyes. He

falls to the ground. He might be dead. Everybody gathers around him.

"Squeaky, Squeaky," I yell. "Can you hear me? Are you dead?" A piece of ice must have been in the snowball because a little trickle of blood runs down his forehead where he's been cut.

Shirley kneels beside me. She shakes his shoulders. "Wake up," she pleads, but Squeaky doesn't move. "Whoever threw that snowball killed my brother," she yells. Mr. Keller runs over. He's supposed to watch us while we play and make sure we don't get hurt, but instead he ignores us and smokes a cigar behind the bus garage.

"Clear a path," he yells. "Out of my way. Everybody, out of my way." He grabs Squeaky by the shoulders and gives him a shake. "Speak to me, Stephono," he commands. "Speak if you're still among the living." Squeaky makes a little squeak. Everyone cheers. He isn't dead after all. Mr. Keller picks him up and carries him into the school. We continue playing until the bell rings. When we get to class, Squeaky isn't there. He has a headache and is lying down on the couch in the principal's office until he feels better. We go to the rest of our classes. Before we know it, the last bell rings and it's time to go home.

Shirley sits in front of me on the bus. She turns around and looks at me. "Thank you for helping my brother," she says and turns her head away from me.

"You're welcome," I say to the back of her head.

"You're welcome," Shirley says to the head in front of her.

"You talkin' to me?" Blew asks as he turns around to look at Shirley.

"No, I was talking to Katie."

"If you're talkin' to Katie, then why'd you talk to me?"

"I didn't."

"Did, too."

"Didn't."

"Shirley was talking to me," I yell to Blew.

"You girls are nuts," he yells back.

"Quiet down back there," Mean Gene yells so we quiet down.

"I was talking to Katie," Shirley whispers.

"Okay, you win," Blew whispers without turning around.

I tap Shirley on her shoulder. "I'm glad Squeaky's okay."

Shirley doesn't turn her head, but she makes the "OK" sign with her long fingers. Her stop's coming up. Mean Gene slows the bus and she and Squeaky get off. Blew and Johnny turn around and look at me. "What day is it?" they ask.

"Robinson Crusoe day. Don't you boys know anything?"

Chapter 22 – Valentines in the Silo

"Did everyone remember to bring an empty oatmeal box for their valentines?" our art teacher, Mrs. Little, asks. "Tomorrow is Valentine's Day and your boxes must be ready. Mr. Quaker will be hidden underneath red construction paper, but I don't think he'll mind. Raise your hand if you brought him in."

Everyone raises their hand except Flint, Blew, and Squeaky.

"Why did you boys forget to bring in Mr. Quaker?"

"We don't eat oatmeal," Flint says.

"Neither do we," Blew lies.

"Same here," agrees Squeaky.

Mrs. Little never yells at us, but she doesn't look very happy as she hears the boys' excuses. "Stephono, your sister brought in Mr. Quaker. You can put your valentines in with hers. Blew, you can share with Larry, and Flint you share with Elizabeth. Now, the first five students in Row One may go to the art table. Everyone else get out a piece of paper and crayons and draw something with a valentine theme."

I'm in Row One with the other smart kids. Rows One and Two are where Mrs. Little put everyone who was good at drawing, but the art table is too small for all of us so the rows take turns. I'm sitting next to Shirley.

"Elizabeth," she whispers. "Flint will think you like him now that he has to put his valentines with yours. Maybe Mrs. Little thinks you like him, too. Maybe that's why she made him share your silo."

"I know, but what can I do?" I whisper.

"Keep the chatter down," Mrs. Little says as she passes out construction paper, jars of paste, dull scissors, and some crayons. "Concentrate on what you're doing. I'll show you how your valentine boxes should look." She shows us how to wrap the paper around Mr. Quaker and paste it so it stays in place. "You may decorate your boxes any way you want, but I'll make the slot in the box top. I don't want you using sharp scissors. You might cut yourself and we don't want that, do we?"

"Why didn't Squeaky bring in Mr. Quaker," I ask Shirley.

"He left him on the kitchen table, Elizabeth. He said he probably wasn't going to get any valentines so there wasn't any reason to bring the silo."

"Everybody likes him so he'll get lots of valentines. Why do you call it a silo?"

"Because oatmeal doesn't come in a box. It comes in a silo."

"You're right, Shirley. You have a silo in your barnyard. What do you keep in it?"

"Silage for the cows and sheep. I wonder why Mrs. Little calls a silo a box."

"Maybe she doesn't know what a silo is. Maybe she's never lived on a farm."

"Girls, less talking and more working," Mrs. Little says as she walks by. "You might need two pieces of paper to cover the entire box," she tells Russell. "Put more paste on the paper or it won't stick," she says to Howard. "That's too much paste," she says to Candy. After criticizing us, she goes back to her desk. We wrap paper around the silo so it will completely cover it. Then we cut out hearts and paste them on. The last thing we do is cover the top. We raise our hand when it's time to make the slot. Mrs. Little takes sharp scissors from her desk and stabs them into the top. When we finish our project, we write our name on it, bring it back to our desk, and practice drawing valentines. The rest of Row One makes their silos, then Row Two. When all the rows have their turn, the silos are lined up on the shelf underneath the window.

Some kids used pink or white construction paper and cut out red hearts and pasted them on the silos. Candy drew an arrow through the heart she made and put CS + HC on it. I know she likes Howard, but he doesn't like her. He put HC + EC on his to let me know he likes me more than Candy or Katie. They're probably mad, but I don't care. He's not very handsome, but he's smart and sometimes it's better to be smart than handsome, at least that's what Momma says.

When the art table is cleaned and everything is put away, it's time for afternoon recess. I don't want to go out because I sneezed three times and told Mrs. Little I have a cold but she said fresh air will do me good. I know I don't have a cold. I just don't want to go out because we always play Red Rover Come Over during second recess, and the boys beat us because they're strong. They break through our arms even when they don't run fast. Boys are like that. They show off for the girls, but we ignore them unless they're cute.

"Red Rover, Red Rover, let Daisy come over," Blew yells. Daisy can't run fast and she's not the least bit strong, but Blew likes her and knows she can't break through. Now she's standing next to him on the boys' side. Russell yells for Katie to come over. She's tall and runs fast. She breaks through and brings Daisy back to our side. I wish she had brought Howard, but girls have to stick together. One day we'll beat the boys and show them who's boss.

When school is finally over and we're on the bus I sit next to Shirley. "It was fun making the valentine silos," I say. "We probably won't have valentine exchange next year. Seventh graders have more work and less fun than sixth graders. And we'll be in the old school. Things sure will be different."

"I know, Elizabeth, but we'll be 12 going on 13 and that's too old to exchange valentines with everyone, but I'll give you one if you give me one."

"Deal," I say. "Daisy told me that Fenders told her that kids in seventh and eighth grades have to stay in the gym after they eat. Girls play jacks on the floor and boys play marbles until the bell rings. There's a concession stand where the twelfth graders sell candy bars and sometimes Popsicles. If anybody throws wrappers on the floor, they're in big trouble. Things sure are going to be different."

"Elizabeth, let's not think about that now. Maybe we'll flunk and won't have to leave grade school. Would you rather flunk and repeat sixth grade with the fifth graders?"

"No way," I say. "We're too smart to flunk. We'd have to fail every course. I might fail music, but one 'E' won't hold me back. Well, here's your stop, Shirley. See you."

"See you, Elizabeth."

After Shirley gets off the bus, Katie sits with me. She tells me about the old school. "That's where we had kindergarten because there wasn't a separate grade school then. Our class was in the basement by the toilets. Our teacher, Mrs. Florence, was strict. Every afternoon we had a snack of bread and peanut butter. Then we had a nap by pushing together three little chairs facing each other. We had school all day because the class was too large for everyone to attend at once. Kids took turns going to school every other week."

"I never heard of anything like that. Sounds like fun. Well, Katie, here's my stop. I better not hesitate or Mean Gene will fly right by my house, and I'll have to get off at Flint's. Then he'll want to walk me home and that will never happen. See you tomorrow." Mean Gene slams on the brakes, and I almost fall out the door.

Chapter 23 – Washington's Birthday

"What special day was Saturday, February 22?" Miss Penny asks.

"Washington's birthday," everybody yells.

"I hope everyone read the handout I gave you on Friday. Now, who will be first to tell the class what you learned about President Washington? Blew?"

"He was the first President of these United States of America. He lived in a big house called Mount Vernon."

"Do you remember anything else about him?"

"He wore a funny hat and his teeth were made from an oak tree."

"President Washington wore what was called a 'Tricorn Hat' because it had three corners. It was the fashion of his time in the 18th century. His teeth were not made from the wood of any tree. That is a fallacy passed from one century to the next. Elizabeth, what can you tell us about President Washington?"

"Miss Penny, can I ask a question?" Flint asks.

"You mean 'may' you ask a question."

"That's what I said."

"What is your question?"

"What's a 'fallacy'?"

"A fallacy is something people believe that isn't true. It's a story that has been told so many times it's taken as truth."

"You mean it's a lie?" Flint can't believe his ears.

"Not really a lie," Miss Penny explains. "Now, let's continue. Elizabeth, please stand and tell us what you know about President Washington."

"He was really tall and he chopped down his father's cherry tree."

"Yes, he was quite tall, but he didn't chop down the cherry tree. That's another fallacy that makes a good story."

"But I read it in our handout so it must be true," Elizabeth argues.

"I made a mistake. President Washington was given a hatchet when he was a youngster. Perhaps he nicked the tree, but he didn't chop it down. Elizabeth, do you know anything else about our first president?"

"His men froze to death during the winter at Valley Forge. He wasn't very nice."

"You'll have to do more reading and learn more about Valley Forge. You may sit down, Elizabeth. Squeaky, what can you tell us about President Washington?"

"Washington owned slaves and he rode a big horse and married a woman because he was lonely and didn't want to live alone in his big house. And he was afraid of the Red Coats."

"Some of what you say is true, Squeaky, but I'd like to think he married Martha because he loved her. I do not think he was afraid of the Red Coats."

"Maybe you made another mistake." Miss Penny ignores him.

"Do any of you know anything about the birth of our nation and the Founding Fathers?" Miss Penny asks. "Did any of you read the handout?"

"I did," Russell says. "Our country was born in Jamestown."

"Our country was born when Columbus found it," Blew says.

"No way," Larry disagrees. "It was always here because my people found it first."

"You mean your dad found America? He'd be so old, he'd be dead. He never lived in Europe, did he? Didn't some queen have a crush on Columbus so she gave him lots of money and some ships to find the United States?"

"There was no United States when the Indians owned the land," Larry says. "It was theirs to roam and different tribes lived in different places. My people, the Chippewa, lived along the shores of Lake Superior."

"Larry's right," Danny agrees. "The Indians were here long before the Europeans came and drove them off their land."

"My folks didn't drive anybody anywhere," Blew argues.

"Neither did mine," Candy and Elizabeth say at the same time.

"Class, Larry gave us some interesting information. You'll learn about the Founding Fathers and the birth of our nation in your history books. Mrs. Messer will answer all your questions. We're discussing President Washington today."

"But don't he belong in history class instead of in English?" Flint asks.

"In a way you're right, but as part of your assignment over the weekend you were supposed to read the handout I gave you about our first president. Did anyone read it?" Nobody raises their hand. "In that case, take it out of your desk and read it now then hand it in. Write an essay on what you remember. You know perfectly well that's why we discuss special days during English class. You're always required to write a report on what you've learned."

"But that ain't fair," Blew complains. "We didn't have to write about Robinson Crusoe. We just read about him and that was a lot more fun. And we never have more than one special day in the month."

"Change is part of life, Blew. Sometimes this year we'll read a book or a handout twice a month. Sometimes only once. Now, get busy reading and writing." The room is quiet as we read the handout. Then we give it in to Miss Penny and start to write. I'm good at remembering so I write fast and raise my hand.

"What is it, Katie?" Miss Penny asks.

"I'm finished with my report."

"Bring it to me." I hand it to her, and she looks it over. "You covered all the main points," she says. "And your punctuation and sentence structure are excellent. Very well done. You may go to the bookshelf and pick out a book and read it while we wait for the rest of the class to finish."

I walk over to the shelf. I've read most of the books, but I see a new one Miss Penny must have just brought in. It's called *Under the Lilacs* by Louisa May Alcott. I loved *Little Women* so I'm sure I'll like this book, too. I read the first chapter and then the bell rings.

"Hand in what you've written," Miss Penny says.

Danny walks beside me as we go to our next class. "You're a fast writer, Katie. And you're smart. I like smart girls."

"Thank you," I say. "You're smart, too. Your parents must be proud of you."

"My dad is but mom doesn't care. She doesn't live with us anymore."

"Did she stay in Paradise?"

"Yes. She's buried there."

"She died?"

"Yes, just before Thanksgiving. She was sick for a long time."

"I'm very sorry. It must be awful not to have a mother."

"Yes, it is. That's why we moved to Brimley. Dad said there were too many memories in Paradise."

"I wish you lived near me. You could come over to my house, and Mama would give you cookies to take home. Where's your house?"

"Right across from the school."

I pat Danny's shoulder as we go to geography class. Mr. Bartlett's pulling down a map of the United States that hangs above his desk. We're learning what each state manufactures. It's interesting, but I can't keep my mind on what he's saying. I'm thinking about Danny going home today. His mother won't be there to greet him and give him a hug and a cookie.

"Katie, Mr. Bartlett says. "Are you daydreaming again? I asked you what Sault Ste. Marie is famous for."

"Sorry, Sir. The Soo is famous for the locks and the carbide and maybe the woolen mill where my aunt worked until it closed."

"Excellent. Who can tell me what other establishments are famous in Sault Ste. Marie?"

"The Alpha Bar and the Antlers," Flint says.

"The Merchant's Bar and Dorothy's hamburgers," Squeaky yells.

Mr. Bartlett shakes his head. "What am I going to do with you people? There's more to the Soo than taverns and restaurants."

"Maybe you could take us on a field trip and show us famous places. We're remembering President Washington's birthday," Flint says. "We could celebrate it by going to one of the Soo's beer gardens or restaurants if we don't find any monuments."

"I give up. You people mystify me." Mr. Bartlett pulls down another map. "This is a map of Europe. Does anyone know anything about European countries?"

"Germany makes beer," Flint yells.

"Ireland makes whiskey," Johnny yells louder.

"Scotland makes scotch," Elizabeth says with a smile.

Mr. Bartlett pulls the strings on the maps and they roll back up. "Get out your geography books," he says. "You people have a long way to go if you intend to pass my class."

Chapter 24 – Shirley Waits with Belle

Today is Saturday and I've been at the barn for hours. I'm waiting for Belle to freshen. She's my favorite cow, and I feel sorry for her because she always has deformed calves. Every year we hope she'll have a normal calf, but when the baby comes out there's something missing or too much of something else and Pap has to shoot it.

My arm's getting tired so I put down the curry comb and sit on a bale of hay. Fuzzy jumps on my lap and starts purring. She has five new kittens. I hope we get to keep all of them. Their eyes are still closed and they look like baby rats, although I've never seen a baby rat. The kittens sleep in a pile and cry when they want Fuzzy. She's a good mother, but I think she gets tired of waiting on her babies just like I get tired of currying Belle.

"You're a good cat," I tell her.

"Shirley, are you in there?" Daisy yells.

"Yes, come in."

"What are you doing in the barn?"

"I'm keeping an eye on Belle. She's going to freshen soon."

"Are you allowed to watch?"

"No, but I'm allowed to keep her company."

"She's got lots of company. All the cows are in their stalls. They'll talk to her."

"I feel sorry for her."

"Why?"

"Because she always has a deformed calf, and Pap has to shoot it."

"Sometimes one of our cows has a freak calf and Fenders shoots it. I sure am glad I wasn't born a calf. He'd have shot me for sure once he saw my club foot."

"Does it bother you that your right foot isn't like your left?"

"I never thought about it until I started school, and some kids called me a freak. When I got home, I told Mama I was never going back because they laughed at me."

"What did she say?"

"She said they'd get used to me. She wrote a letter to the teacher. I don't know what it said, but by the end of the week most of the kids were limping like me so I wouldn't feel bad. I made lots of new friends."

"None of the kids on the sideroad laughed at you. We were always your friends."

"That's true, but sometimes I wish the doctor could heal my foot."

"I wished that last year when Belle had a calf with only three legs. The Pickford vet is old so Pap didn't call him, but the Rudyard vet is young. He might have had an idea, but Pap shot the calf as soon as it was born."

"Poor Belle. I hope she has a normal calf. Will you let me curry her?"

"Yes, but be careful. She has dung in her hair." As soon as Daisy starts currying Belle, she puts her head in the manger and pulls out a flake of hay. She shakes her head and chaff flies everywhere. I sneeze. Belle drops the flake. She turns her head and looks at us. "My friend is currying you," I tell her. "You'll feel better when she gets some snarls and dung off. That's a good girl."

"I'm trying not to hurt her," Daisy says. "I curry our cows and they don't like it, either. Winter is hard because they have to stay in the barn. They get dung on their side when the lay down."

"I know. If we didn't curry them, they'd be an awful mess come spring. Belle knows you're trying to help her. Daisy, do you ever think what it's like to die?"

"No. Do you?"

"Yes. I think about death all the time."

"Why?"

"Because we live on a farm and death is all around us."

"Katie told me about the dead kittens you found. I'm sorry."

"I still have nightmares about them, and now Fuzzy has a new litter. I don't want them to die, but Mom says we have too many cats and all newborn kittens have to go."

"You can give me one, maybe two and maybe Johnny will take one. Maybe Blew and Candy and Elizabeth. Then they'll all have a home and won't have to die."

"You're a good friend, Daisy."

"You are, too, Shirley. Let's go sledding tomorrow while the snow is still good." Daisy hands me the curry comb.

"I think I'll go home now," she says. "See you tomorrow."

"Bye, Daisy. Thanks for talking to me." Just as she leaves, Pap walks in. He's carrying milk cans.

"How's Belle doing?" he asks as he checks her over.

"Okay, I guess. Do you think it will be soon?"

"Won't be long now," he says and starts milking.

It's quiet in the barn except for the squirt of milk falling into the pail, one squirt tumbling after another, making a one-two, one-two sound. After each cow, Pap gets up and pours the milk into a tall can. Then he picks up the stool and milks another cow. He leans his head against the cow and seems lost in thought. His wavy hair has gray patches around his ears. His beard is dark brown with strands of gray going through it. The most beautiful blue eyes I've ever seen belong to Pap, and he's so handsome we hardly notice his missing front tooth. It fell out when he was young and stepped the wrong way on a hoe. It smacked him in the mouth. Mom wants him to get the tooth fixed. He says he will later, but later never comes.

Sometimes I wonder if Mom likes Pap. I've never seen them hug or kiss, and they don't hug Squeaky or me either. It doesn't seem natural not to hug someone if you love them. I hug Fuzzy, and I hugged the dead kittens even though they couldn't feel it. I decide to ask Pap something I've wanted to know for a long time but never had the courage to ask. My back is to him.

"Pap, do you love me?"

He keeps milking and says in a quiet voice, "That's a strange question, Shirley. Why do you ask?"

"You never tell me you love me."

"There's a lot of ways to say 'I love you' without actually speaking the words. Do you know what I mean?"

"No."

"Do I ever spank you?"

"No."

"Do you have more chores than Squeaky?"

"No. Do you love me more than Squeaky?"

"No, I love you both the same, but Squeaky is stronger and can handle more work around the farm than you can."

"Will he get the farm when you die?"

"Not all of it. You'll get 50 acres and so will your brother."

"Who gets the house?"

"Don't worry about the house," Pap says. "You'll be married with a home of your own. Maybe even a farm of your own. You won't need the old house."

"But what if I don't marry? What if nobody wants me, and I'm an old maid?"

"Then the house will belong to you and Squeaky until one of you marries."

"You didn't answer my first question. Do you love me?"

"Yes, Shirley, I love you more than you'll ever know."

Before I can ask anything more, Mom opens the door. She's carrying a plastic bowl full of apple peelings. Her face is white from the wind, and her eyes are watering. Her lips are bright red. She always wears red lipstick, even to the barn. She hands me the bowl.

"See if Belle will eat these," she says. I dump the peelings into Belle's feedbox. She noses them and picks some up. Mom loosens the scarf around her neck and turns on the radio that's on a shelf. It's turned to WSOO, the local station. The guy's playing a sad song, something about coming home because it's suppertime. I'm starting to get hungry. Mom runs her hands along Belle's middle like she's feeling for something. "I don't think it will be too long now," she says. "Time for you to go to the house."

"But I want to stay."

"No, it's time to go." Mom's voice tells me not to argue. "I'll be back in a few minutes," she says to Pap. "I'll bring Squeaky with me."

"Why does Squeaky get to help, but I don't?"

"Because he's a boy and you're a girl. It's not proper for a girl to watch a cow give birth."

"Why not?"

"Because I said so."

When we get to the house, Mom tells Squeaky to stop playing with his toy soldiers and put on his barn jacket. Then she tells me to get a couple of bowls for the stew simmering on the stove. She says Gram and I are to eat supper and wash the dishes. Then she and Squeaky go to the barn. The stew smells good. I hand Gram a bowl, and she fills it with lots of peas and carrots but not much meat because she knows I don't want to eat one of our beef cows that might be in the stew. Gram fills her bowl and pours each of us a glass of milk.

"Gram," I say. "Do you ever think about dying?"

"Sometimes. Why do you ask?"

"I was thinking about Belle's calf. It will die if it's deformed, won't it?"

"Yes, I'm afraid it will."

"Do you think there's a heaven for animals?"

"I think they have spirits, and when they die their spirit flies off to heaven where they wait for us to join them when we die."

"Do you think we share heaven with animals?"

"Yes."

"Do you think Belle's calves are waiting for us or is heaven only for cats and dogs?"

"I think every animal that dies is waiting for us."

"Even the mice and rats?"

"No, those are rodents. I don't think rodents have spirits."

"I don't think so either. This stew is good."

"Yes, it's very good. Shirley, I don't want you to worry about Belle. If she's meant to birth a healthy calf, she will. If not, there's nothing we can do about it."

"I know, Gram. It's out of our hands, isn't it?"

"Yes, my dear. It's out of our hands."

After we eat, I wash and dry the dishes and put them in the cupboard. Then I get out my Shirley Temple coloring book and sit at the table and color. Gram sits on her cot and continues knitting a pair of mittens. It's quiet in the kitchen except for the tick-tock of the clock. It's warm in here, too, and there's a feeling of peace. I love our house even though we don't have running water and a bathroom like Elizabeth has. The first time she came here, I thought she was snooty. She didn't even want to see my dolls. Maybe she thought I was crazy playing with dolls at my age, but I won't be 12 until next month. That's when I'll have to pack them away. Mom explained I'll be a young lady then, and young ladies do not play with dolls. I get sad thinking about it so I try not to. I continue coloring. It isn't long before the kitchen door opens and Mom walks in.

"Is Belle okay?" I ask. "Is her calf born?"

Mom smiles as she takes off her jacket and washes her hands. "She's fine," she says. "Belle has a healthy little calf. You can see them now if you want to."

"Is it boy or a girl?"

"A girl and she's beautiful."

I throw on my jacket and boots and run for the barn. When I open the door, I can't believe my eyes. Belle's licking her baby.

"She really is beautiful," I whisper.

"And she's healthy," Pap says. Squeaky agrees.

"Can I name her?" I ask.

"What do you want to call her?"

I think for a minute. "How about 'Apple?' I'm sure it was the peelings that helped her get born."

"'Apple' sounds like a good name," Pap says. "What do you think, Squeaky?"

"Yup. 'Apple' it is."

Pap finishes milking the rest of the cows and carries the cans to the wellhouse. Squeaky uses the manure fork to clean the stalls. He puts the manure and dirty straw in the wheelbarrow and wheels it out to the manure pile where he dumps it. Then he spreads clean straw for the cows' bedding. When he finishes, he sits on the bale of hay next to me.

"Pretty little thing, isn't she?"

"She's beautiful," I say.

"Belle sure loves her."

"She's happy because she has a healthy baby."

"Well, Shirley, I'm going back to the house. Don't stay out here too long."

"I won't," I say, but I have no intention of leaving until I make sure Apple is licked clean and has a full tummy of Belle's milk. When Belle lays down and Apple snuggles next to her, I wipe happy tears from my eyes. Now I can leave the barn. When I step outside, the air is cold and crisp. I'll never forget this day. Pap loves me and Belle birthed a healthy calf. Even if I live to be 100, I'll never forget the happiness I feel right now. I wish I could feel this way forever.

Chapter 25 – The Wearing of the Green

"I ain't got nothin' green to wear today," Blew complains as he slams our front door. "Not even a snot rag. Nothin'. What'll I do?" He throws his jacket on the floor, sits next to Grandpa, and whines like a whipped dog.

"There, there," Grandpa says. "The pipes burst at school so you're not going anywhere today except to the barn to do your chores. It doesn't matter if you wear something green or not. The cows won't notice if you're not wearing a shamrock."

"But, Gramps, that ain't the point. I'll know. I let down poor old St. Patrick again. Last year the 17th was on a Sunday. All I had was one lousy green sock to wear to church. Nobody saw it. Even Johnny looked like a Christmas tree."

"You're crazy," I say. "Put on your jacket and help me bring in some wood."

"No, Katie. I'm stayin' right here next to Gramps."

"Okay, crybaby, but just wait. The next time you ask for help with story problems, I won't lift a finger." After announcing my threat, I march out the back door and head for the woodpile. One of my chores is bringing in armloads of wood for the kitchen stove. I mutter to Lard as I stack wood on my arm.

"Blew's an idiot. Papa says we don't have to wear green if we stay home." Lard barks. I think he understands every word I say. I pound on the door and Blew opens it. "Well, it's about time. What took you so long?"

"It didn't take a minute," he says. "Is that all the wood you got?"

"If you weren't so lazy, you'd help, and the woodbox would be full by now. You're lazy and dumb and useless." I jab him with a little piece of birch. He howls like Lard does when he bays at the moon.

"You poked me," he cries. "I think you made me bleed."

Mama takes a pan of cinnamon rolls out of the oven. "Are you two fighting again?" she asks. "What's wrong now?"

"Nothin'," Blew lies.

"Nothing," I say.

"Blew, help Katie fill the woodbox. When you finish, the cinnamon rolls will be waiting for you."

If there's one thing Blew loves it's Mama's cinnamon rolls slathered with gobs of butter. He grabs his jacket and beats me to the door. He forgot all about the little jab I gave him. Boys are just big babies. When I get outside, he's playing fetch with Lard. A lot of help he's going to be.

"Get over here and help me," I command. He ignores me.

"Here Lard. Come here, boy. That's a good dog." Lard brings the stick and drops it at Blew's feet. He throws it farther this time. Lard runs fast as lightning and brings it back. Blew throws it past the wellhouse. He has no intention of helping me.

"If you don't help me with the wood, you won't get any rolls," I threaten. "I'll tell Mama all you did was play with Lard." Blew pretends he didn't hear.

"Good boy. That's a good dog. Almost as good as Utah. Go fetch," he says. The stick sails past the wellhouse and lands near the pigpen. The pigs come running because they think they might get some slops. Sometimes pigs are as stupid as boys.

"Lard is ten times smarter than mangy old Utah," I yell. "Your dog's headed for the bone pile. He won't last until spring." Whenever I make fun of Utah, Blew gets mad. Now he's running towards me. I run up the porch steps and pound on the door. "Let me in. Blew's after me." Mama opens the door as Blew turns around and runs toward the woodpile.

"I'll be right there," he yells. "I'm lookin' for big pieces." He makes a show of digging through the sticks. He knows they're all the same size so they'll fit in the stove.

"Blew won't help. He's playing fetch with Lard."

"I know," Mama says.

"He's dumb and lazy."

"I know."

"If you know then why don't you make him help me?" Just then the door opens and Blew comes huffing and puffing in with wood piled almost to the top of his head.

"That's why," Mama says and winks at me. We finish filling the woodbox then throw snowballs at each other. The snow is packy so we roll it until we have the beginning of a snowman. Yesterday Blew and Johnny came over and made three balls, but they didn't stack them. They froze to the ground during the night so now they're useless, and we have to start over.

"You're doin' it all wrong," Blew yells. "You ain't makin' a ball. You're makin' a lumpy mess. Git in the house 'cause you don't know nothin' about makin' a snowman." He pushes me out of the way and mutters something about it takes a feller to know how to make something out of snow.

"Be that way," I yell. "You and Johnny were too scrawny to stack the balls yesterday. You made them too heavy. All you did was keep rolling snow until you couldn't push it anymore."

"Git," Blew yells and throws a snowball at me. He misses as I run for the house.

"You won't last five minutes before you'll be crying your fingers are frozen." I go inside and hang my jacket behind the stove. In a minute, Blew's back in the house doing the same. We sit on the bench with our backs to the wall. Mama brings a plate of rolls, two glasses of milk, and the butter dish. She pours a cup of tea for herself and Grandpa. We sit around the table and listen as Grandpa tells a story.

"When I was a boy in Ireland," he says. "My mother always wove green ribbons in my sweater. I remember one St. Patrick's Day I was sick and couldn't go to church. When everyone was gone, I slipped out of bed, found some ribbons, and wrapped them around my wrists. Then I prayed to St. Patrick to make me well."

"Did he?" Blew asks. His eyes are round as saucers. Everyone knows Grandpa tells tall tales.

"He sure did. By the time my parents and brothers got home, I was fit as a fiddle and dancing a jig with a leprechaun."

"Are leprechauns real?" Blew asks. He's staring at Grandpa like he's the smartest person in the world.

"Oh, yes. As real as that roll in your hand. As real as a four leaf clover."

"Did you ever see one when you lived in Ireland?"

"Yes, many times. They were everywhere. I had to be careful not to step on one when I walked. They hide in the tall grass." Grandpa stirs milk into his tea and takes a sip. He smiles a special smile that means he knows I know he's teasing, but Blew doesn't know. At least I don't think he does. You never know with boys.

"Do you think leprechauns live in Brimley? Did they hide in your pocket when you sailed across the ocean? What do they eat? Where do they sleep? Do they have pots of gold at the end of a rainbow? If I find one can I take it to school and show the other kids?" Blew asks Grandpa a dozen questions. His story gets longer and more ridiculous as he answers each one. When Blew asks if St. Patrick really charmed the snakes out of Ireland, Grandpa says that was way before his time so he can't say for sure. He tells Blew to look it up in the *World Book Encyclopedia.*

"I will as soon as I get home," Blew lies. That's a fib almost as big as Grandpa's leprechaun story. Blew never goes near an encyclopedia. He buttons his jacket, sticks a roll in his pocket, and runs for the door. "Thanks for the grub," he says.

"Watch out for leprechauns," I warn. "You're not wearing anything green so they might attack you." I laugh as I slam the door behind him. Then I peek out the window and see Flint. He's yelling at Blew so I open the window and listen. The boys are up to something, and it usually means trouble. Mama tells me to close the window. I lower it, but I leave a little crack open so I can hear what they're saying.

"Hey Blew, wait up," Flint yells. "I got something in my jacket pocket to show you that you ain't gonna believe." As soon as I hear that, I slam down the window, put on my boots, grab my jacket, and head for the door. I tell Mama I'll be right back. When the boys see me, they tell me to scram. Flint says, "I got something to show Blew, and it ain't none of your business. Get back in the house."

"I'm not going anywhere," I say. "You're in my yard."

"Well, then I'll get on the road. C'mon, Blew. You're gonna love this." The boys run across the road down the lane leading to Blew's house. I run after them.

"Go home," they yell, as if I'm a dog. Just then Johnny comes down the road on his horse. For once, I'm glad to see him.

"Johnny," I yell. "The boys are being mean. Help me." Johnny reins in Butterball and smiles like he's looking at an angel. Maybe I made a mistake. I sure don't want him to think I like him because I can't stand him most of the time. I think I see stars in his eyes as he jumps off Butterball and hands me the reins.

"Hop on," he says. "I'll catch up with the boys. We'll meet you at Blew's house. They won't be mean to you when I get through with them." He lopes away as if he's part Arabian. I'm not a very good rider, but I put my foot in the stirrup, grab the pommel, and hoist myself up. Butterball's gentle. She walks like an old woman. She walks slower than Grandpa when he walks with his cane. When I get to Blew's house, I tie the reins around a fencepost and head for the kitchen. Aunt Mags is frosting a cake with green icing.

"Hello, Katie," she says as I take off my boots and jacket. "Happy St. Patrick's Day. Where's your shamrock?"

"I don't have to wear one today because I'm not going anywhere."

"I always wear green on this special day," Aunt Mags says. "It's to remember the miracle of St. Patrick."

"I guess you're right." I'm beginning to wish I'd stayed home. For sure I'm not going to see what Flint has hidden in his pocket because the boys are in Blew's room, and I wouldn't go in there for a million dollars. And now Aunt Mags is making me feel guilty for not wearing anything green. "I'm going home," I say. I reach for my jacket, but before I put it on we hear a crash upstairs.

"What's going on up there?" Aunt Mags hollers. "Why all the racket?" She looks at the ceiling as if she can see through it.

"Nothin'," the boys yell.

"Nothing my foot," Aunt Mags yells back. She heads for the stairs and clomps up them. I follow her and stand by the bottom step and listen. The boys are in trouble for sure.

"Unlock the door this minute," she says. I hear a click. Then I hear her scream. "What are those varmints doing in your room? Get them out this minute. Do you hear me?" I think anyone who isn't dead can hear her, but I keep quiet. Just then two green rats run down the stairs. I scream as loud as my aunt. Utah's resting by the stove, but when he sees the rats, he comes to life as if somebody jabbed him with a hot poker.

The chase is on. The boys run down the stairs. Aunt Mags is right behind them. They run after Utah as he runs after the rats. Rats are horrible things, and I'm staying out of the way. I sure don't want a green rat running up my pants leg. That stupid Flint is always making trouble, but I never thought he'd do anything as crazy as this. Everybody knows rats carried the plague that killed all the people in Europe. Aunt Mags continues to scream and shout orders. Utah corners one rat behind the kitchen woodbox. Flint grabs the other by its tail and swings it around his head. Uncle Marvin walks in the front door as Flint lets go of the rat. It flies through the air and just misses my uncle's head.

"What's going on here," he demands. "Have you all gone crazy?"

The rat hits the wall and knocks itself out. It's laying on the floor and looks like it's dead. We run over to it. Flint picks it up and cradles it in his hands like it's a precious baby kitten instead of a dirty green rodent. "Poor little Ratty," he coos. "Poor little thing. Are you still alive?" He puts the rat next to his ear and listens. "Yup," he says. "I hear his ticker going strong. He's gonna make it. Where's his brother?"

"Utah's got it cornered behind the woodbox," Johnny yells. Every time the rat sticks its head out, Utah grows and barks, and the rat goes back to its hiding place. Flint walks over and pushes Utah out of the way. He takes a piece of bread from his pocket and in a second the rat grabs it. Then he grabs the rat and sticks him back in his pocket.

Uncle Marvin is madder than Aunt Mags. "Whoever brought these rats into my house is going to get a whipping," he shouts. "Flint, are they yours?" Flint doesn't say a word.

"Blew? Johnny? Katie? These rats belong to one of you? You might as well fess up and get it over with." Nobody says a word. Then Aunt Mags covers for us.

"They're mine," she says. We can't believe she's lying to protect Flint. She doesn't even like him. "I found them in the woodpile and felt sorry for them," she explains. "I painted them green in honor of St. Patrick. Flint, since you caught them you may take them home."

We grab our boots and jackets and run outside. We laugh until tears streak our cheeks. Whoever thought Aunt Mags would lie to protect a boy. I guess we'll never understand her, but we're sure glad she did. Otherwise Uncle Marvin would have grabbed Flint by the ear and whipped him good.

Blew goes back to the house. Johnny lets me ride Butterball home. When I get off, Johnny jumps in the saddle and pulls Flint up behind him. I wave to the boys. We had a good laugh, but I sure hope I never see another green rat as long as I live. Not on St. Patrick's Day or any other day of the year.

Chapter 26 – Mrs. Eel Goes Away

"Does anyone know why Johnny missed school this week?" Mr. Bartlett asks.

"His mom ran away and she ain't coming back," Flint says.

"What do you mean?"

"She ran away with the preacher from Kinross. Everybody's talking about it. Ma says it's the biggest scandal to hit the county since Mr. Roi had too much to drink and ran over Mr. Sims' finest Brown Swiss cow and landed in jail."

"Flint, are you telling me the truth?"

"I ain't lying. Ask anybody."

"We won't discuss this any further. Open your textbooks to Chapter 9. It's time we learned how rocks are formed."

"But I thought you wanted to know why Johnny's not here," Blew says.

"Rocks, people. We're going to discuss how sandstone rocks are formed. Our area, especially Sault Ste. Marie, has many buildings made from sandstone quarried locally. Elizabeth, stand and read the first five paragraphs. People, pay attention."

And that's what we did during class, but Mr. Bartlett couldn't stop us from discussing Johnny on the bus ride home. "Poor Johnny," Elizabeth says. "I saw him Saturday riding Butterball, and, Katie, he was crying."

"Did he say anything?" I ask.

"No, not a word. I pretended I didn't see his tears. I talked about my horse. I yakked on and on. Johnny told me I was lucky because my dad's a captain of a ferry boat, not a pig farmer like his dad. Then I told him my real dad raises beef cattle in Dafter. He always smells like barn. That's why Momma divorced him, moved to Mackinac Island, and married the Captain."

"What did Johnny say to that?"

"He said my mother took me with her. He said Captain must have wanted me. I told him that whether he wanted me or not Momma wouldn't marry him unless I was with her. That's when Johnny started crying really hard and didn't even try to hide his tears."

"What did he say?"

"Katie, he told me when he got home from school last Friday his pa was making toast. When he asked where his ma was, his pa said she was gone, and they were on their own. Johnny asked if she had gone to the Soo or Brimley, but his pa said no, that she was just gone and wasn't coming back. Then he made two pieces of toast for Johnny and called it supper. Then they went to the barn and milked the cows and fed all the pigs."

"Did she really run away with a preacher?"

"Yes, Katie, and he didn't want Johnny. He said the boy's place was with his pa, at least that's what Johnny said he said."

"It's sad to think of Johnny without his mother. I think I'd die if Mama left with a preacher and I never saw her again. I'd absolutely die."

"I'd have died if Momma had left me with dad. I love him and will spend July with him and my stepmother and Ronnie, but a girl's place is with her mother. Well, here's my stop. Come over tomorrow if you want to. Bye Katie."

"Bye, Elizabeth." I can't believe Johnny's mother won't be living with them anymore. He was so happy a couple weeks ago when the boys had fun with Flint's green rats. I wonder if he'll ever be happy again. Everybody likes Johnny. I know he likes me, but I like Howard, at least I think I do. I never see him during summer because he doesn't live on a farm in the country. Mean Gene slows the bus for my stop.

"Mama," I say when I get in the house. "You won't run away with a preacher will you?"

"No, of course not, Katie. Are you thinking about Johnny? Was he at school today?"

"No, he missed all week. I feel sorry for him."

"The best thing you can do is be kind to him when he returns to school," Mama says. "Don't ask questions. He's probably very sad."

"Katie, come sit by me." Grandpa pats the kitchen chair next to him. "He's going to need good friends. Just treat him like you always do. You know what happens when you fall and skin your knees?"

"Scabs form."

"That's right and what happens if you keep picking at them?"

"They bleed and take longer to heal."

"That's right. A broken heart's the same way."

"You miss Granny, don't you?"

"Yes, Katie, I miss her every day." The phone rings in the living room, and I go answer it.

"Katie, is that you? Danny here."

"Yes, it's me. What do you want?"

"I called Johnny, but he wouldn't talk to me."

"What did you call him for?"

"I wanted to tell him my mother died so I know what it's like not to have one."

"That was nice of you, but it's not the same."

"I know. Well, bye."

"Bye, Danny."

Later that evening when I'm walking from the barn, I see Johnny riding Butterball. I wave. He waves back and turns down my lane. "Is everybody talking about me?" he asks.

"Yes, but not in a mean way. We're your friends."

"Will you ride with me?"

"I'll ask Mama and be right back." I run to the house. "Mama says I can, but only to the end of the road. We can't cross M-28."

Johnny stretches out his hand and pulls me up behind him. We walk down my lane and turn left. There's still a lot of snow on the road and a few patches of mud where it melted. He guides Butterball so she stays on the snow. Johnny doesn't say anything until we turn the corner. Then he makes Butterball walk even slower.

"I don't understand why she left," he says. "I always minded her, and I almost made the honor roll last marking period. I promised her I wouldn't quit school and join the Army like my brothers did. What'd I do wrong, Katie, to make her run away?"

"You didn't do anything wrong. It didn't have anything to do with you."

"That's what Pa says. I wish I could believe him, but I can't. I must have done something awful to make her run away."

"You didn't do anything wrong," I repeat.

"Maybe it was the pig farm. She hated those pigs. She hated the smell and the noise they made when we scalded them."

"Johnny, maybe one day she'll come home and tell you what it was. I guess you'll have to wait until then."

"You're a good friend, Katie." I lean my head against his bony shoulder as he turns Butterball around and we head back to my house. He's a nice boy. I think I could like him more than I like Howard if it wasn't for the pigs. They squeal and grunt and sometimes a sow will crush one of her piglets when she rolls on it by mistake. I would never marry him, though. Not unless he sold all the pigs and bought goats instead. They can be mean, but at least they don't smell like hogs.

Chapter 27 – Larry's Birthday Party

Captain's takin' us to Bay Mills for Larry's birthday party. Our next stop is Candy's. "Run faster," I yell. "Captain's revvin' the motor. We're gonna leave you if you don't step on it."

"Blew, stop teasing her," Daisy says. "She's running as fast as she can."

"Take my hand," Flint offers. "I'll pull you up."

"Take my hand," I say, but Candy already has both her hands in Flint's as he pulls her onto the truck's bed.

"Thanks, Blew," but Flint's hands were the first ones I saw. What's the hurry? I thought we had plenty of time before the party."

"We do have time. Flint just wanted to hold your hands." Candy doesn't say anythin' but she looks at Flint like he's Pat Boone. She sat with him on the bus every day last week. I don't think Squeaky has a chance of winnin' her. He ain't gonna like Candy sittin' next to Flint, but there ain't one thing he can do about it. Squeaky and Shirley are waitin' for us at the end of their lane. I help Shirley. Squeaky hoists himself up.

"Where do we put our presents?" Shirley asks. Elizabeth taps Captain's window. He rolls it down, and she hands him the presents.

"Everybody aboard?" he asks.

"Aye, aye, Sir," we yell.

"Ahoy, mates. Batten the hatches and hang on. The wind's blowing hard and the seas might be rough, but we'll make it through if we pull together." Captain likes to talk in ferry language. When we get to Brimley, we cross the bridge and keep goin' until we're on the reservation where Larry lives. He's waitin' on the porch for us.

"I thought you'd never get here," Larry yells. "I got a fire going down by the lake." Captain goes in the house. We run to the shore.

"Wow," Elizabeth exclaims. "This is beautiful. I've never seen lake ice breaking up."

"It sure is somethin'," I agree. "It looks like the pictures in our geography book. It's not like river ice. Larry, you sure are lucky to live here. I wish I lived along the shore of Lake Superior."

"This is Indian land, Blew," Larry explains. "If you were Indian, we might be neighbors. You guys like the fire? I made it myself and put birch stumps around so we'd have something to sit on."

"Your presents are in the truck," Elizabeth says. "Where do you want us to put them?"

"Leave them in the truck for now. After we roast hot dogs and marshmallows, we'll go inside. Ma baked a cake and made ice cream. Thanks for coming, guys."

"What do you think of my lake?"

"It's beautiful," Elizabeth sighs. "I've been to Alcott Beach lots of times, but I've never been there when the ice was breaking up. This is amazing."

"You sure are lucky, Larry," Squeaky says.

"We Ojibwes knew all about Lake Superior before the white man came. We fished and canoed and learned its ways and thanked it for its bounty. Chief's told me lots of stories about when he was young. Things were different then."

"Will you tell us some stories?" Katie asks. "We don't know anything about Indians except that a lot go to school, but many quit when they turn 16. You won't quit, will you?"

"I don't know," Larry answers. "First I gotta get through the rest of this year then seventh and eighth grades. I won't be 16

until after my freshman year. If Chief needs me to help with net fishing, I might quit. If not, I might keep going until I graduate. I'd be the first in my family."

"Why do Indians quit school?" Elizabeth wants to know.

"Maybe because we have a different idea of schooling," Larry says. "We learn things important to us. Do you know the names of those trees over there? Or that low-growing bush? Or the birds flying above us? Or those clouds floating by? Do you know how to make a strawberry basket from the strips of a black ash tree? Or how to bead a necklace? Or how to make a quill box from the quills of porcupines? Or how to recognize sweetgrass?"

"No, I never even heard of strawberry baskets or sweetgrass."

"We have egg baskets and timothy grass we make into bales of hay for our cows, but I never heard of sweetgrass," Katie says. "Do you eat it?"

"No, we burn it."

"As fuel?" Blew asks.

"No, Blew, we burn it before ceremonies."

"Why?" inquires Johnny.

"To get rid of bad spirits."

"Does it burn the spirits?" Katie is curious.

"No, we smudge the air and that chases the evil spirits away."

"How do you smudge air with burnt grass?" Shirley asks.

"You don't understand our ways. Smudging is when the sweetgrass has been bound or braided. We cut off one end, light it, and the smoke purifies the air."

"Won't the grass burn your hand?" Johnny asks.

"No, the grass is green so there's no flame. Only smoke. When the purifying ceremony is over, Chief puts out the flame by tapping it in the sand."

"What does sweetgrass smell like?" Elizabeth inquires.

"It's sweet," Larry says.

"Will you burn some for us?" I ask.

"No, Blew, it's only for certain ceremonies."

"Like what?"

"Like never mind. You ask too many questions."

"Are there evil spirits here?" Elizabeth sounds scared.

"They're everywhere," Larry says.

"Are they in those little boxes over there?" Daisy points to a graveyard.

"That's Indian burial ground from a long time ago. My great-grandfather's over there. Those boxes are called 'spirit houses.' White people don't know much about Indians except what they see on television shows like Roy Rogers or the Lone Ranger."

"Most white people don't understand our ways. Chief says when people don't understand something, they call it dumb or stupid, but it's just different, that's all. He says we have to be patient, and one day people might understand us."

"Why do you call your dad 'Chief'?" Shirley inquires.

"I got that idea from Elizabeth when she called her stepfather 'Captain.' I think it's a good idea, and Chief likes it. Now all my brothers and sisters call him 'Chief.' Even Ma. She calls him the 'Big Chief.'"

"Does he wear feathers in his hair?" Katie asks.

"No, we don't wear ceremonial dress anymore."

"Why not?"

"I don't know. Hey, the fire's burning low. There's a stack of dry birch in the woodshed. Follow me and we'll grab some logs. Get some little sticks, too, so we don't smother the flames."

"That'll put out the fire, and all we'll get is smoke, right?"

"You're right, Blew. You might have some Indian blood in you after all. Don't cover all the coals. That's where we'll roast our dogs and marshmallows."

We grab small birch logs. Larry shows us how to put them on the fire so it won't go out. I've never been to his place before, but I have a feelin' I'll be back this summer even if I have to hitchhike. Learnin' how to be an Indian is a lot more fun than learnin' about the Russians and the Cold War and the Space Race and sandstone rocks. And Larry's better than any of our teachers. I think he's smarter, too, 'cause he ain't never been to college, but he knows all about Indian ways. He don't have to read about 'em in a book.

His mother comes out with a tray of food. We roast the dogs where the coals are. When the wind blows smoke in Shirley's face, she brushes it away until Larry says smoke always finds the prettiest girl and settles on her. I roll my eyes. I guess that's his way of tellin' Shirley he likes her. After we eat, we go in the house and watch Larry open his gifts while we eat cake and ice cream.

Lots of kids had birthday parties this year, but this is the best one ever. Finally it's time to go home. We thank Larry and his parents for invitin' us. They tell us we're welcome to come back anytime.

"That sure was fun," Flint says when we're on the road again. "I learned a lot. Maybe I'll quit school when I'm 16 and become an Indian."

"You will not." Candy's voice is firm. "Not if you want to be my friend. You'll go to college, too, and become an astronaut and fly to Mars."

"That's a lot of trouble," Flint groans.

"Girls are worth it."

"Maybe. Maybe not."

"You sound like Fenders," Daisy laughs.

"Sure do miss him," I say. "Why'd he join the Army?"

"Well, Blew, Daddy said it was either the Army or the jailhouse so Fenders had no choice if he wanted to be free. He's in Germany now. He says he likes the Army. They let him drive a big truck. He only wrecked it once."

"He sure was an awful driver," I agree. "He never should of left the cornfield." Everybody laughs. April 1st has been a mighty good day. Nobody got April Fooled, at least not as far as I know unless Larry was foolin' us about smudgin' evil spirits and them spirit boxes. He said the little holes in the top was to let the spirit of the dead out. Gives me the willies just thinkin' about it.

"All hands to your muster stations," Captain yells. "And batten the hatches. There's rough seas ahead." We hear him laugh as he rolls up the window. I think Captain wishes he was captain of a big freighter on Lake Superior. Nobody knows what a muster station is, but we know we're supposed to answer by yellin' aye, aye. That's what we do as we head towards home.

Chapter 28 – Yellow Chickens

"Katie, you goin' eat all them yellow chickens?" Blew asks. He's poking through my Easter basket. He's already eaten all my black jelly beans, the ears off my chocolate bunny, and three marsh-mallow eggs.

"Go home," I say. "Go eat your own yellow chickens. You know they're my favorite." I pop another Peeps in my mouth. I love the hard sugar coating and the soft mushy inside. Daisy's still in her new Easter clothes, preening around like a pink rooster in the barnyard.

"You can have all my yellow chickens," she says to Blew. "But only if you give me all your pink jelly beans and promise to bring them to my house."

"No problem," Blew says. "Pink's for sissies and I sure ain't one. I'll bring 'em over tomorrow." Blew winks at me. We all know by tomorrow his basket will be as empty as an August bird's nest. Daisy knows it, too, so I don't know why she's willing to give up her Peeps unless it's because she likes my cousin. Before we can argue anymore, Mama walks in and tells Daisy and me to set the table.

"Is Jewel Red Nails goin' eat with us?" Blew asks.

"Yes," Mama says. "But please don't call her by that ridiculous nickname."

Jewel Red Nails is an old lady who lives in a cabin in the woods behind our house. Her long fingernails are always painted red. Jewel visits Grandpa almost every day. They were friends in the old days. She usually brings gifts. One time she gave Granny a ball of purple yarn and gave Grandpa a compass that only pointed south. She's given me lots of presents, but the best one was a string of plastic pull-apart beads. Last October she gave Papa an empty wasp's nest that kept flaking apart. At Thanksgiving she gave Mama a jar of sourdough starter. We never know what she'll pull out of her pockets.

"Jewel Red Nails is crazy," Daisy says. "Look at all the nutty getups she wears."

"She's not crazy, just different. I like her funny outfits," I say.

"Katie, who wears all the clothes they own at the same time?" Blew asks. "The kids at school don't do that. Imagine a boy wearin' three pairs of overalls or a girl wearin' all her dresses. They'd look ridiculous just like Jewel does."

"You always take Daisy's side. And how do you know how many clothes the kids have?"

"Well, I don't, but you know what I mean. Don't act stupid."

"Blew's right," Daisy says. "Don't act stupid."

"Are you girls going to help me?" Mama calls to us. Daisy and I head for the kitchen. Blew stays in the room. I know he's going to steal as many of my Peeps as he can stuff in his pockets.

The kitchen smells good. There's a ham in the oven, potatoes boiling on the stove, and although I can't smell it, I know there's a coconut cake decorated with jelly beans in the pantry. As we're setting the table, there's a knock on the door. Grandpa opens it and in walks Jewel Red Nails.

"Happy Easter," she hollers. She gives Grandpa a kiss on his lips, shakes hands with Papa, and hugs Mama. Then she throws her arms around Daisy and me and almost knocks us down. She hugs Aunt Mags, Uncle Marvin, and Daisy's parents. She smells like peppermint. She's wearing so many clothes she looks like a clown except she doesn't have floppy shoes.

"Come in, come in," Grandpa welcomes her. "Come sit by the fire. You must be cold after your walk. Eva, pour Jewel a cup of tea." Grandpa barks out orders like a sergeant. Jewel laughs as she unwinds her long scarf and takes off two pairs of mittens, two hats, one thin jacket, one coat, and a pair of men's boots. I know I shouldn't stare, but I can't help it. I've never seen anybody wear so many clothes. Maybe Daisy's right. Jewel Red Nails might be crazy.

"See what I brought you," she says. "Come here, Katie, and put your hand in my pocket." I stick my hand in the pocket of her long black dress. I feel something soft and fluffy and then I feel a sharp peck.

"Ouch," I say and withdraw my hand. Jewel laughs and pulls out a little yellow chick and then another and another. She holds them in the palm of her hand.

"They're beautiful," I say, and she gives me one. The little chick turns its head and looks at me. I hold him gently. He's so tiny he's almost lost in my hand.

"I brought a chick for you and Blew and Daisy," Jewel says. "And a couple more for good luck." She reaches in another pocket and pulls out two more chicks. They make peeping noises as she sets them on the table.

"Not there!" Mama yells. "Katie, get a shoebox from upstairs. We can't have these little fellows running all over our dishes. Watch out! Grab him before he runs into the butter!" But it's too late. One chick sticks its beak in Mama's fresh butter. Another runs around the sugar bowl. One hops on Papa's plate. Jewel grabs the chicks and stuffs them back in her pockets. She and Grandpa laugh. I look at Mama. There's a smile on her face so now everybody laughs because we know Mama's not mad.

Blew hears the commotion and runs to the kitchen. "What's all the fuss?" he asks. When Jewel shows him the chicks, he lets out a hoot. "Yellow chickens for supper. If that don't beat all!"

"You idiot," I say. "We're not going to eat them. We're never going to eat them are we Mama?"

"No, Katie. We'll keep them as pets and remember this Easter as the day Miss Jewel brought us the perfect gift." I run upstairs and get a shoebox. We poke air holes in it and place the chicks in the box. They keep peeping, but I know they're safe. Blew grabs his jacket and runs to the barn for a handful of hay and some mash from the chicken coop. We put that in the box along with a little saucer of water and put the box behind the stove where it's nice and warm. Soon the peeping stops as the chicks fall asleep.

It isn't long before Johnny and his dad arrive. Mama invited them to join us. She's always baking bread or cookies, and Papa takes them down to Mr. Eel and Johnny. When everyone is sitting at the table, Papa says grace and Mama passes around the food. Everything tastes good. There's a lot of talk and laughter, and we're having a good time. When the meal is over, Mama brings out the cake and everyone claps. After dessert, Blew runs from the table and takes the shoebox from behind the stove.

"Johnny, wanna see some real yellow chickens?" he asks as he opens the box. "I ain't never gonna eat another yellow Peeps again without seein' these little critters."

"Will that stop you from eating all the yellow Peeps in my Easter basket?" I ask.

"Shucks, no, Katie. There ain't nothin' gonna keep me away from your basket." He and Johnny run to the living room. I run after them.

"If you give me all your Peeps, I promise I won't let nobody chop off another chicken's head as long as I live," Blew lies.

"Promise?"

He looks me straight in the eye. "I sure do," he says. "Cross my heart, Katie. Now, gimme them Peeps and throw in some jelly beans."

I know he's lying, but I do as he commands. I don't care about some silly candy chickens when I have the real thing behind the stove. Johnny taps my shoulder. "I brought you a chocolate egg," he says. "I bought it with my chore money." He hands me a flat egg wrapped in crumpled paper. He must have sat on it while we ate. I sure don't want it, but I can't hurt his feelings.

"Gee, thanks Johnny. Do you want a marshmallow bunny?" He nods. I don't want to give him one, but I guess I have to. Now he'll think I like him, but I don't think I do.

"Hey, how come you give him candy, but I have to beg for some?" Blew demands to know.

"Because Johnny isn't a liar like you."

"I'm goin' home," Blew grunts. "And Johnny's comin' with me." They grab their jackets and the adults tell them not to get into trouble. From the window, I see them run to our shed and get out the fishing poles. Then they run down the road towards the river not towards Blew's house. As usual, he lied.

Jewel is standing next to me. She watches the boys. "Johnny likes you," she whispers in my ear. "That boy is head over heels."

Now I know for sure she's crazy. Nobody in their right mind would accuse boys of being head over heels about anything except toy guns, dump trucks, plastic cowboys, and catching fish.

"What about me?" Daisy asks. "Do you think Blew is head over heels about me?"

"Yes, indeed," Jewel says. "Yes, indeed."

"How do you know for sure?"

"Because he looks at you just like Katie's grandpa looks at me."

"Does he love you?" I can't believe my Grandpa loves Jewel.

"Katie, he's loved me since we were young."

"Then why didn't he marry you instead of Granny?"

"Well, dear, that's a long story. Maybe one day I'll tell you, but not today. Run along now and play."

"Do you think your granny stole your grandpa from Jewel?" Daisy asks when we're setting up the checker board.

"I don't know."

"Maybe one day they'll get married now that your granny's in heaven."

"Maybe. What color checkers do you want?"

"Red, my favorite color. It must be Jewel's too. I wonder if she paints her toenails."

"I don't know. Let's get the game going and forget about the old people."

"They sure are funny," Daisy says.

"I agree. We never know what they're thinking."

"Do you think we'll be like them when we get old and gray?"

"No, Daisy, we'll have more sense. We'll never wear all our clothes at once or carry five chicks in our pockets. And we'll certainly never kiss an old grandpa on his lips. It's your move."

"I can't imagine kissing anyone on the lips except maybe Blew," Daisy answers. "He doesn't tease me about my club foot. He says it makes me special because no one else has one."

"He's not so bad," I say. "But keep your mind on the game or I'm going to win." I hope Blew isn't lying about Daisy's foot. I don't think he is. He's a liar, but he's not cruel. "Good move," I say. "You might win this time, but I'll win the next game."

"Maybe. Maybe not," Daisy says.

"You sound just like Fenders." We laugh and get on with the game. Later, when Jewel Red Nails is ready to leave, Grandpa grabs his cane. We watch as he takes her hand. Maybe she will be my new grandma. She'll never replace Granny, but she'll be lots of fun.

"Your move," I say. "Better make it a good one or I'll win."

Chapter 29 – A Late April Snow

Candy and I are walking from the barn when suddenly snow begins to fall. The flakes aren't like winter snowflakes that are so big they look like pieces of paper somebody tore up and threw out a window. April snowflakes are tiny and sparkle as they float around us. They look like miniature stars and disappear as soon as they touch the ground.

"Katie, look at the beautiful snowflakes," Candy says. She lifts her face that is soon dotted with tiny droplets. Then she sticks out her tongue, and snowflakes immediately melt on it. All around us the sky is filled with diamonds. "Snowflakes are turning the sky into a fairyland," she says. "Quick, Katie, catch some on your tongue before they're gone." I stick out my tongue and that's what we're doing when Johnny, Blew, and Flint run down my lane.

"Are you girls crazy?" Flint asks.

"You know they are," Blew says. "All girls are crazy."

"You're wrong, boys," Johnny disagrees. "They're not crazy. They're having fun. Everyone knows the last snow of April is special."

"Stick out your tongue, Johnny," I say. "Catch as many flakes as you can. Make a wish and it will come true. That's what my Granny always said before she died and went to heaven."

"You guys look stupid," Flint grunts. "There ain't no magic in any kind of snow or we'd all be magicians with the amount of snow we get. You guys are nuts. C'mon, Blew. Let's get out of here."

"I believe Granny is sending these snowflakes to tell me she loves me and will never forget me even though she's busy in heaven," I say.

"Have it your way, Katie," Flint snaps. "But we're outta here. Are you coming, guys?" Blew follows him, but Johnny stays with us.

"Ever since Mom left, I keep hoping she'll come back," he says quietly. "Maybe catching snowflakes will be the miracle that will bring her home."

"Maybe," I agree. "It sure would be wonderful." Johnny sticks out his tongue and catches a few flakes, but then he stops.

"I guess I'll join the guys. See you later." He yells to Blew and Flint. We watch them race towards the river.

"Do you like Johnny?" Candy asks.

"I don't know. Maybe. He's changed a lot since his mother ran away."

"But what about Howard? You still like him, don't you?"

"I don't know. I never see him except at school, and he almost never talks to me. He doesn't call me, either, even though I gave him my phone number. Mama says his dad's a bigshot at the Air Force Base in Kinross. Maybe Howard's a bigshot, too."

"Don't you like bigshots?" Candy asks.

"I don't like anybody who thinks they're better than I am. Remember I told you what Shirley told me? That when Elizabeth first visited her she wouldn't drink the cows' milk or play with Shirley's dolls? Elizabeth was a stuck-up bigshot, but since she's gotten to know us, she's okay."

"But Elizabeth hates dolls. She only likes horses."

"Shirley told me her mother is making her pack all her dolls in a big box and put them away. Now that she's 12, her mother says she's too old to play with them. I think Shirley's sad. She cried when she told me."

"Parents sure are funny," Candy says. "Flint's pa ran away two years ago. Johnny's ma ran away this year. Elizabeth's ma smokes cigarettes. Howard's pa is a bigshot. Larry's pa burns sweetgrass. Shirley's ma won't let her play with dolls. Danny's ma died. Blew doesn't have a pa or ma, only grandparents. My ma won't let me wear lipstick even though she has hundreds of Avon samples from Daisy's mother. What's wrong with your ma and pa?"

"They make me go to church every Sunday and Holy Day of Obligation."

"What kind of day is that?" Candy asks.

"It's like a special day in our church."

"Like somebody's birthday?"

"No, like the day a saint died or something like that. You can have Howard now that I don't want him anymore."

"Thanks, but I don't want him either. He gave me a lousy valentine. Remember? It was meant for a boy. I might like Russell, but I'm not sure. He's awfully shy. If he lived on our sideroad, I'd see him during the summer, but Eckerman might as well be a thousand miles away."

"Maybe you could call him."

"I can't call a boy. It wouldn't be right."

"Hey, look. It stopped snowing. The magic's gone. We might as well go in the house. Mama's teaching me to bake. Maybe she'll let us bake cookies."

"Okay," Candy says. "I'll call Mommy."

"Tell her you'll take home a batch of chocolate chip cookies."

"Good idea."

The sun comes out as we run to the house. Now that the snow has stopped, the magic's gone. I don't believe what Granny said. I don't believe catching April snowflakes on our tongue will make a wish come true, but sometimes it's nice to pretend especially if it makes a friend feel better. I don't think anything will make Johnny's mother come home because his pa still has all the pigs. If he got rid of them, maybe she'd come back, but who knows? Parents are a lot more complicated than kids.

Chapter 30 – JEP, Mama's Special Gift

For Mother's Day, Mama wanted a piglet so Papa bought one from Johnny's pa. I watched as Johnny picked up the little pig, dropped him in a gunny sack and held it while Papa tied a piece of binder twine around the top. Then he paid Mr. Eel, and we got back in the truck. The piglet squealed and squirmed between Blew and me.

I felt sorry for the little pig, but Blew laughed. "Katie, you're too softhearted," he said. "You gotta toughen up." I ignored him. It was the first time piglet was away from his family, and he was scared. Anybody would be scared if somebody plucked them from their pigpen, dropped them in a sack, and put them in a truck between two kids who didn't know the first thing about how it felt to be snatched from a pen and trapped in a sack going heaven knows where.

I named him JEP which means Johnny Eel's Pig. He cried all the way home. Blew held him tight when we got out of the truck because he was wiggling and trying to get away. Papa didn't put him in the pigpen with the big pigs because they might eat him so we put him in the old chicken coop we don't use anymore. He cried for a long time until he fell asleep. He probably knew there was nothing he could do, but when Papa went to the barn this morning, JEP was gone. I was upstairs when Papa came into the kitchen. I heard his voice through the stovepipe.

"Your pig got out of the coop and is nowhere to be seen," he told Mama. "He must have gone home. I'll hop in the truck and drive to Eel's."

I ran down the stairs and out the door. Before Mama could stop me, I was in the truck with Papa. When we got to Johnny's, nobody was around except the dogs so we walked to the pigpen without waiting for someone to greet us. The big red sow was feeding eight piglets, one of which was too big to nurse. It was JEP. Papa told me to get the gunny sack.

Johnny and his pa came from the barn. Papa and Mr. Eel had a good laugh about the runaway pig. Papa picked him up and put him in the sack and tied the top. I hopped in the truck and held the sack. Papa drove to our barnyard gate, and then he took the sack and put JEP back in the coop. Mama had left some breakfast scraps and milk for him, but he didn't even stick his nose in the dish. He just squealed.

"What are we going to do?" I asked. "Will he die if he doesn't stop? Should we take him back until he's older?" I peppered Papa with questions.

"Katie," he said. "It won't take JEP long to learn he has a new home and can't keep running back to his old one. He'll squeal for awhile, but he'll settle down and be okay." The door opened and Mama walked in. "Do you need help?" she asked. Papa grabbed JEP so he wouldn't escape and handed him to Mama. "Here you go," he said. "Happy Mother's Day."

Mama smiled and wrapped her arms around JEP. "What's the matter, little fellow?" she asked. She spoke in a sing-song voice. "There, there now," she said. "Calm down. That's a good boy." She rocked him in her arms and kept talking in a gentle voice until he stopped squealing.

"You sure have a way with animals," Papa said. "Granny would be proud if she could see you now." JEP was nestling in Mama's arms like a newborn baby.

"That's why I wanted a piglet," she explained. "As a reminder that new life is all around us."

I sat next to Mama on the bale of hay. The morning sun was shining through the window, Papa was spreading fresh bedding on the dirt floor, and I was thinking about all the fun JEP will have rolling in the mud once he's big enough to live in the pigpen. Everything was peaceful until Blew pounded on the door.

"Is it safe to come in?" he hollered. "Has that dang old hog quit screechin' or have you killed him?" Blew pushed open the door. "Well, I'll be," he said. "If that don't beat all. What a picture. Aunt Eva, you look like Mary holdin' baby Jesus. I wish I had a camera. Shove over," he commanded me and plunked down next to Mama. He stroked JEP's back. The piglet snuggled closer to Mama, but he didn't seem to mind Blew's dirty hands as he rubbed grime into his bristly hair.

"Looks like you've woven your magic around him," Papa said. "I have a feeling JEP is going to like his new home now that he has three nursemaids."

"I ain't no nursemaid," Blew yelled, but he kept petting JEP. He didn't fool me for one minute. Mama smiled like she was the happiest person in the world. Like she knew the secret to happiness had nothing to do with money or pretty clothes or anything else except being around the people who love you. Maybe she was remembering what Granny used to say, that love in your heart is worth more than all the money in the bank. That without it, the richest man in the world is poorer than a pauper. Now I know why Mama wanted a piglet for Mother's Day. The best gifts are the ones we share with others.

Chapter 31 – Saying Goodbye to Miss Penny

"What special day was yesterday, May 11?" Miss Penny asks.

"Mother's Day," everybody yells.

"Excellent, class," she says. "But it was also another special day for a very different reason. Remember the story I read to you on Friday? Howard, please stand and tell us why May 11, 1953 was a special day."

"It was the day the *Steinbrenner* sank in Lake Superior and everyone drowned."

"The Great Lakes freighter did sink, but not all the sailors died. Some were rescued by other ships in the area. Who remembers how many sailors were saved?" Russell raises his hand, something he hasn't done all year. "Russell, will you tell us?"

Russell stands as tall as a beanpole. "Seventeen brave sailors went to their watery grave that day. Now they're in Davy Jones' locker where they'll spend the rest of their lives. Today is a special day, too, because it's almost our last day in sixth grade English class, and we'll never have to learn about special days ever again." He sits down and everyone claps.

"Thank you, Russell. You are right. Today is special in more ways than one. Before we discuss the *Henry Steinbrenner*, how many of you have enjoyed learning about special days?" Nobody raises their hand so I raise mine. "Daisy, tell me why."

"We learned lots of special dates in Mrs. Hubbard's class but too many to remember, and they weren't interesting. I learned more about history in English class than I did in history class because you told us why the days were special."

"History is full of important dates," Miss Penny says. "Mrs. Hubbard didn't have time to explain in detail why each date was special."

"Do you have more time than Mrs. Hubbard?" Flint asks.

"Not more time, Flint. Perhaps I find some special days more interesting than others. Now, who can tell me what happened to the *Steinbrenner*?" Kids start yelling answers. Some say it went down because its load of iron ore was too heavy, and the ship was caught in a strong gale and sunk like a stone. Elizabeth says one of the hatches came loose, and the captain sent an SOS before he told the crew to get in the lifeboats and abandon ship. "Class, you remembered more about this special day than any other one. Why do you suppose this is?"

"My grandpa was a sailor," Russell explains. "I forget which ship he sailed on, but I know it didn't sink because he died a couple years ago when his heart gave out."

"I think it's because we're surrounded by water. Even when we go to the Soo, we have to cross a bridge to get downtown," Candy suggests. "I guess Sault Ste. Marie is really an island."

"I liked the story of the *Steinbrenner* because I like to read about shipwrecks on the Great Lakes," Flint says. "Once I read about a ship that sank in Lake Michigan. She was carrying a cargo of Christmas trees. Nobody in Chicago had a tree that year, but for years afterwards those old trees kept washing up along the shoreline."

"The *Rouse Simmons* was a schooner," Miss Penny replies. "It was called the 'Christmas Ship' and her captain was called 'Captain Santa.' All the trees had been cut from Upper Peninsula forests. Perhaps some people had a tree to decorate for the Christmas of 1912, but you're right, Flint. Most did not."

"How do you know so much about ships, Miss Penny?" I ask.

"Because, Daisy, my father was a sailor for many years."

"Did his ship sink?"

"Not when he was a Merchant Marine. My father died during World War II when his ship, the *USS Reuben James*, was struck by a torpedo." The room gets very quiet. Miss Penny walks over to the window. There's a shelf full of books underneath it. She pulls one out. "Flint, have you read this book?" she asks.

"Yes, I took it home before Christmas vacation."

"I don't remember giving you permission."

"I didn't ask for permission. I just took it."

"Why did you choose it?"

"Because it's about shipwrecks on the lakes. I'm sorry I didn't ask permission."

"Is this the only book you borrowed without asking?"

"Yes, honest. It was the only one that looked interesting."

"Would you like more books on shipwrecks?"

"Yes."

"I'll bring you some tomorrow," Miss Penny promises.

"That's great. Thanks."

"Miss Penny, what ship did your father sail on?" I ask.

"He sailed on many different ships. Some were freighters that sailed in salt water off the coast of Florida. These ships were called 'salties.' He sailed on the Atlantic and Pacific Oceans. He sailed all over the world, Daisy, thank you for asking."

"That must have been exciting. Was he a captain?"

"No, he didn't want that responsibility. When he was on the freighters, he shoveled coal in the engine room. When he was in the Navy, he was a lieutenant."

"Will you tell us about his adventures?" Russell asks.

"Not today. Today you must write about the *Steinbrenner*. I want complete sentences and paragraphs. Remember all the rules you've learned about proper grammar and punctuation. Make sure your spelling is correct."

Everybody groans. We want to hear about Miss Penny's dad and his sea adventures. He must have had plenty. I wonder if he saw a whale as big as Moby Dick or if pirates boarded his ship and stole the cargo. But instead of asking questions, we get out notebook paper and start writing. My pencil needs sharpening. I walk by Miss Penny's desk to get to the sharpener that's nailed on the wall beside her.

"Miss Penny," I whisper. "I'm sorry your father died." She doesn't say anything but reaches for my hand and squeezes it. Then she takes a Kleenex from the box on her desk and wipes away a tear trickling down her cheek. I look the other way. I didn't mean to make her cry, but I guess I'd cry, too, if my Daddy was at the bottom of the ocean instead of home putting a new fence around the milk cows' pasture.

When the bell rings, we hand in our reports. "I'll miss all of you," Miss Penny says. "You've been excellent students. The best I've had in many years." We tell her we'll miss her, too. Then we hurry out the door to our next class. I hope she doesn't start crying again but if she does, I hope she has a full box of Kleenex tissues in her drawer.

Chapter 32 – Apple's Fate

Blew and I dangle our legs over the edge of the haymow and watch Apple nibble at the grass in the pasture nearest to the barn. We have one more day of school. Summer stretches before us like a hill that has no end but goes on and on, up and down forever. After we ate the pieces of cake Mom gave us, we climbed the ladder to the haymow. Now we're looking at the fields and watching Apple.

"Well, Shirley, Apple sure is a pretty little thing," Blew says. "Yup, she'll bring a good price when she goes to market in the fall." He takes his jackknife out of his pocket and scrapes cake from underneath his fingernails.

"Don't say that, Blew. Pap won't sell her."

"Sure he will. A farm's gotta make money or go under."

"Pap says there's more to farming than just making money. He says you got to love everything about it or find another job."

"Everybody knows you can't live without money. Love ain't got nothin' to do with nothin'. I'm goin' home if you're gonna talk about love." Blew closes his knife and jumps from the mow. "Bye," he says. "See you later."

I watch Apple walk farther down the field, following Belle. Once the calves are weaned, they're allowed back in the pasture with their mothers. I'm always glad about that because I know they're happy. When Pap separates them, the calves cry and their mothers bawl and the noise is awful. I know it has to be done because the calves would drink all of the cows' milk. If that happened, we wouldn't have any milk to sell and wouldn't have any money. Without money, we'd land in the poorhouse. But now I'm worried. If Pap sends Apple to auction, I'll be sad knowing people are going to eat her. She's very pretty and gentle, and she came from a milk cow so she should be safe because when she's older Pap will milk her, too. She's all gray except for a splash of white between her eyes. I think it looks like a star, but Blew says it looks more like a piece of broken glass.

I reach for my satchel hanging on a nail. Like Katie, I always keep a coloring book and crayons handy so I have something to do when I sit in the mow. As much as I try to concentrate on what I'm coloring, I keep thinking about Apple going to auction. Mom says I worry about everything, but so does she.

"Shirley, where are you?" Squeaky yells. "Candy's here. We're gonna ride our bikes to the corner. Wanna come with us?"

"No."

"Good. It'll just be me and Flint and Candy. Maybe Elizabeth will ride her horse along with us. You'd never be able to keep up without collapsing." I watch as they pedal down the lane and head for Elizabeth's house. The end of the sideroad is two miles away. The fields are full of trees. Some are alive and healthy, but others are dead and look like monsters that might jump out and wrap their branches around me. I imagine lots of things that never happen. Things like trees coming to life as people who died a long time ago. I imagine the limbs are their arms, and they're trying to grab me. It scares me just to think about it. I go back to coloring. It isn't long before I hear Katie.

"You up there?" she yells.

"Yes, I'm here. Climb up."

"You still like to color?"

"Yes, but don't tell Mom. She'd say coloring is for kids."

"I know what you mean," Katie agrees. "It's hard being 12. It's like we're in between. We're not kids anymore, but we're not teenagers either. Where is everybody?"

"They went for a bike ride."

"Why didn't you go with them, Shirley?"

"You know I don't like that stretch of road with the dead trees on both sides. I never ride there because it scares me."

"Me, too," Katie says. "Let's ride towards the river. There are no dead trees that way."

"Okay." I put away my coloring book and crayons. "Want to jump down? Blew always jumps, and he's never broken an arm or leg. Let's do it and see what happens. Close your eyes and jump."

"Let's hold hands." Katie reaches for mine.

"Okay, here goes." We fly through the air. "That wasn't bad," I say as we hit the ground.

"You're right. It's no big deal. Want to do it again?"

"No. Once was enough for me. Let's get our bikes and go." As we pedal down the road, I tell Katie what Blew said about Pap sending Apple to auction. "I sure hope he doesn't," I say.

"I don't think he will, Shirley. He loves you too much to do that. Apple will stay with you until she's an old cow and dies on her own."

"How do you know my Pap loves me?"

"Because every father loves his daughter."

"Hey, wait up," Blew hollers as we start down the road. "I'll ride with you gals."

"Eat our dust," we yell. "Eat our dust."

"You're a lot more trouble than you're worth," he says, but he pedals fast and catches up with us.

"If we're so much trouble, then why do you want to ride with us?" Katie asks.

"'Cause there ain't nobody else to ride with. I'm stuck with you two."

"Could be worse," I say.

"You could be right, Shirley," Blew agrees. "But I wouldn't bet on it." He laughs as he pedals like the wind, sails past us, and disappears down the hill.

Chapter 33 – No More School

It's the last day of school. I'm in no hurry as I walk down the lane. As usual, I said goodbye to the house, and as usual, Ma and my sisters were asleep. Jazz and Jill are still mad at me because I grabbed the feed sack before they could get it. I think Candy liked her Christmas present, but it's hard to tell with gals. They lie all the time. Pops didn't come home or send a gift for Christmas or my birthday. Ma baked a cake, but I didn't have a party. She said birthday parties are over now that I'm 13. I sure wish I hadn't flunked kindergarten. I'm the oldest kid in our class and the tallest.

I learned a lot this year. I don't fight with Squeaky anymore. It's nice to have friends and be invited to their house to play or just fool around with their dogs. I don't have a dog. Ma says she'd end up caring for it. I promised I would, but I'll be gone all summer. The relatives in Pickford and Rudyard argued over who would get me first. I'm a good worker, and I'm strong so they all wanted me. I'll help plant the gardens, weed, and work with the livestock. When it's time to take off the hay, I might get to drive the tractor.

Sometimes Candy sits with me when she gets on the bus. I've held her hand a couple times so I know she likes me. I hope she doesn't forget about me while I'm gone. I asked Blew to keep an eye on her. He promised he would, but he likes Daisy so he probably lied. I'll ask Squeaky. He doesn't have a girlfriend. He says they're too much trouble. He might be right because Daisy made Blew promise to stop saying "ain't" and stop dropping the "g" at the end of his words. She said she'd fine him a dime every time he spoke in the old way. I sure am glad Candy didn't make me promise anything.

Elizabeth and Danny are friends. I think they're both stuck-up because their dads aren't farmers. Pops never farmed anything more than chickens, and they don't count. Everybody has chickens, even the people who live in town. Captain's always driving Elizabeth over to Danny's house and visiting with his dad. She tells everybody Danny's house is almost as beautiful as hers. Who cares about a house? Pops always said it doesn't matter whether you're rich or poor as long as you've got a good heart. When I was younger, I thought he meant a healthy heart, but now I understand.

Katie told Johnny she'd help him with his chores and maybe bake him some cookies. I knew it would happen. The more she said she didn't like him, the more I knew she did, but she wouldn't admit it. She told Candy she could have Howard, but Candy didn't want him so maybe Shirley will take him. You never know what girls are thinking. One minute they like you. The next minute they ignore you.

All-in-all the school year was a good one. I never thought I'd say this, but I'm going to miss it. I'm not looking forward to seventh grade. We'll have to take lots more subjects, and Miss Penny won't be our English teacher. She was awful nice to me. She kept her promise and gave me some paperback books to keep. She said I'd like them, and I believe her. I'll miss those "special days" as she called them. They made history come alive even if we did have to write a report in class so she could make sure we followed proper English rules. Yesterday she told us she's going to teach history next year because Mrs. Hubbard is retiring.

I'll miss Larry, too. He told us a lot about Indian life. It was fun going to his birthday party. He showed us some Petoskey stones and something he called "Yooperlites" that glow in the dark. Nobody had ever seen anything like them. He'll spend the summer helping the Chief catch whitefish and what they don't sell, they'll cook over a campfire. I sure wish I lived along Lake Superior's shore. I'd swim in the water every day no matter how cold it was. Then I'd fish and have supper and sleep in a tent.

I hear the bus turn the corner. Mean Gene isn't mean if we obey his rules. He doesn't step on the gas anymore when a kid gets on. He used to do that all the time, and the kid might fall in

the aisle. Everyone laughed. I stopped laughing the day I landed on my face. It's no fun when the joke's on you.

"Good morning, Flint," Mean Gene says. "I bet you're glad it's the last day of school."

"Morning," I say. "I guess so, but I'll be working for the relatives and that means up with the chickens and working all day in the fields."

"Could be worse, boy. Could be worse," he says. Then he closes the door and waits until I take my seat in the sixth row. I like to sit by the window. I watch the trees whiz by as we go up one hill and down the other. We've just crossed the bridge so the next stop will be Candy's.

"Did you hear that Howard broke his leg last night?" she asks as she sits next to me. "He won't be in school today."

"What happened?"

"Elizabeth said he was climbing that big elm tree in Danny's yard and he fell. Danny told him not to climb it, but Howard was showing off for the girl who just moved to their neighborhood. She's from Drummond Island. We won't meet her until next year. She'll be in our grade."

"Seems like this year went by awful fast," I say.

"Seems that way, Flint," Candy agrees. Then Daisy gets on.

"Move over," she says. "Did you hear about Howard?"

"Yes," Candy replies. "He called Danny last night and Danny called me. Howard's in the hospital. He asked Danny to clean out his desk and give all his stuff to Russell."

"What if Russell doesn't want it?" I ask.

"I suppose we'll take what's left. Howard's desk is full of stuff."

"Does he have a protractor?"

"I don't know, Flint," Daisy says. "Maybe. Maybe not."

"You sound like Fenders," Candy laughs. "Is your brother still in Germany?"

"Yes."

"Does he like the Army?" I ask.

"He says it's better than jail, Flint."

"Everybody out," Mean Gene yells as he pulls into the schoolyard. He opens the door and kids pile out. Teenagers head for their school to the left of ours. It's so old some of our parents went there. Ma made it to ninth grade before she quit to help my grandma who was sick. If I keep going, I'll be the first person in my family to graduate high school. Kids in grades kindergarten through sixth head for our school. It's only two years old, and there aren't any stairs. The old school has plenty of them. Some go down to the basement, and some go up to the second floor. I hope I find the right rooms next year for all my classes.

"I hope the new girl doesn't laugh when she sees my club foot," Daisy says. "I wish I had feet like everyone else."

We're almost at our homeroom door. Mrs. Lark is smiling and waiting for us like she's done all year. "It's not your foot that's important," I hear myself say. "It's what's in your heart that's important." The words sound silly once they're out of my mouth, but I'm only repeating what I've heard Mrs. Lark say a million times. I hope it's true because sometimes teachers tell us lies to make us feel good. I guess that's just the way things are. Candy squeezes my hand like she's proud of me. There's no way she's gonna forget me this summer.

"Welcome, children," Mrs. Lark says. She closes the door and hands out bags of candy. "I'm going to miss each and every one of you."

"We'll miss you too," Blew says. Everyone claps. Principal Jackson opens the door and sticks his head in.

"What's going on in here?" he demands. "Why all the racket?"

"Don't you know?" Mrs. Lark asks. "It's a special day, Friday, May 23rd, the last day you'll see all these wonderful children."

"Well, in that case, carry on," he says. "I probably won't need to use the paddle today." He closes the door and everyone, even Mrs. Lark, laughs. For sure, the last day of school is gonna be a good one.

Glossary

Babe the Blue Ox: A fictional Minnesota folklore animal who turned blue during the winter of the blue snow.

Cargo: What a ship carries from one port to the next.

Centennial Dress: An old-fashioned dress with lots of layers of material.

Club Foot: A human foot that from birth is twisted out of shape.

Cows' Milk: Milk that comes straight from the cow and is not pasteurized.

Dipper: A small tin drinking vessel with a long handle.

Duluth: A city in Minnesota on Lake Superior with the largest and busiest port on the Great Lakes.

Dunce Cap: A tall paper cap with a pointed tip students were forced to wear in class if they didn't know the answers when the teacher called on them.

Feed Sack: A cloth sack containing grains. The cloth was often made into towels or clothing.

Folklore: Fictional stories passed from one generation to the next.

Freighter: A large ship that carries cargo.

Freshen: A term used when a cow gives birth.

Gordie Howe: A famous Canadian hockey player.

Haymow: the part of a barn where hay is stored

Headdress: A headband with beads and feathers.

Jackie Gleason: A comedian who always threatened to send his wife to the moon.

January Thaw: A warm temperature in January.

Laid Out: A deceased person who is waked in his/her own home.

Leprechaun: In Irish folklore, a tiny fairy that gets into mischief.

Mars Bars: A chocolate candy bar.

Merchant Marine: A person who sails on a ship carrying cargo instead of passengers.

Muster Station: A place on a ship where sailors gather for safety.

Nancy Drew: A fictional detective character created by author Carolyn Keene.

Paddle: A long, narrow piece of wood used by teachers to spank children as punishment for disobedience. Sometimes holes have been drilled in it.

Paul Bunyan: A Minnesota fictional folklore character.

Pauper: A person who has no money.

Petoskey Stone: A pebble-like rock with fossils.

Poor House: A place where people go when they have no money.

Port: The destination of a ship.

Protractor: A plastic math instrument used to measure angles.

Red Rover: A children's game played outdoors.

Silage: Dry grass used as animal feed.

Silo: A round, metal farm structure where grain or silage is stored.

Soo Locks: Located in Sault Ste. Marie, MI, the locks are a series of waterways that allow ships to navigate different water depths by raising and lowering the ship.

Sow: A female pig.

Sputnik: An artificial Russian satellite that was the first to orbit the earth.

Statue Maker: A children's game where one player twirls another and whatever position that child lands is how he/she is supposed to stay.

Stutter: The inability to say certain words without repeating the first letter.

Tenners: Tennis shoes/sneakers.

Victrola: A large phonograph cabinet for playing records at a speed of 78 rpm.

Wake: Keeping watch over a deceased person.

Yooperlites: Rocks in Michigan's Upper Peninsula that appear to glow under a UV light.

About the Author

The author resides on the land of her youth near the country town of Brimley in Michigan's Upper Peninsula. She's surrounded by childhood memories and a way of life that is no more. Instead of relying on intricate plots and schemes, her stories are driven by the characters and their interactions with each other, their teachers, and their parents. The authenticity and innocence of the kids will remind adults of days gone by.

Ms. Kennedy writes a weekly newspaper column for *The Sault News* and the *Cheboygan Tribune*. She authored *Life in a Tin Can*, a random collection of previously published columns. Her work also appears regularly in the *U.P. Reader*.

CPSIA information can be obtained
at www.ICGtesting.com
Printed in the USA
BVHW070724110921
616364BV00007B/161

9 781615 996032